The Mover of Bones

FLYOVER FICTION

Series editor:

Ron Hansen

The Mover of Bones

ROBERT VIVIAN

University of Nebraska Press   Lincoln & London

Library of Congress
Cataloging-in-Publication Data
Vivian, Robert
The mover of bones / Robert Vivian.
p.   cm.—(Flyover fiction)
ISBN-13: 978-0-8032-4679-9 (alk. paper)
ISBN-10: 0-8032-4679-X (alk. paper)
1. Janitors—Fiction.
2. Nebraska—Fiction.
I. Title.   II. Series.
PS3572.I875M68   2006
813′.6—dc22
2005037103

Set in Minion by Bob Reitz.
Designed by Roger D. Buchholz.

This book is dedicated to
Meredith Phelan, without whom it would have never been written—

Ladette Randolph, whose brave bright seeing brought
this book to the light—

My wife, Tina, for her constant love and support—

My mother, who taught me how to spell when I was sure I couldn't—

And to all those whose sons or daughters
or loved ones are missing.

The hand of the Lord was upon me, and he brought me out by the
Spirit of the Lord, and set me down in the midst of the valley;
it was full of bones. And he led me round among them; and behold,
there were very many upon the valley, and lo, they were very dry.
And he said to me, "Son of man, can these bones live?" And I
answered, "O Lord God, thou knowest." Again he said to me,
"Prophesy to these bones, and say to them, 'O dry bones, hear the
word of the Lord. Thus says the Lord God to these bones: Behold,
I will cause breath to enter you, and you shall live. And I will lay
sinews upon you, and will cause flesh to come upon you, and cover
you with skin, and put breath in you, and you shall live;
and you shall know that I am the Lord.'"

EZEKIEL 37:1-6

And when he had entered, he said to them, "Why do you make a
tumult and weep? The child is not dead but sleeping." And
they laughed at him. But he put them all outside, and took the child's
father and mother and those who were with him, and went in
where the child was. Taking her by the hand he said to her, "Tal'itha
cu'mi"; which means, "Little girl, I say to you, arise."
And immediately the girl got up and walked, and they were
immediately overcome with amazement.

MARK 5:9-42

Contents

The Mover of Bones

Das Lied von der Erde

The night Jesse Breedlove found the bones it was raining and he was drunk. They were the bones of a small girl, perfectly intact, under three feet of hard clay in a church cellar in Omaha. The clay was covered with fine silt, like an outermost membrane of dust.

He had wandered down there wildly, careening back and forth on the drafty stone steps, the rain sweeping behind him like a veil and the swinging metal door clanging in the lashing wind, sending him downward, cursing and laughing in the rage of his isolation. He threw his jacket down in the corner. He shuffled around, making a half-circle, looking for a place to start digging, muttering to himself.

In one hand he held the shovel, in the other a bottle of Cuervo Gold. He put the bottle down hard on the rough edge of the worktable, making the amber liquid swing in its cradle like the eye of a lantern. Then he set to work.

   Sweetie pie, come down to die, come down to die—

He worked his fury into the end of the pointed spade; it bit and bit, its rounded edge digging up half-moons of clay.

A stone gallery of statues watched him dig: the Virgin Mary incarnated into a dozen different shapes, sizes, and ages, with complexions white as eggs or dark as Mexican girls'; St. Joseph with his flock of ceramic birds and sheep that lay coiled and grazing in a pasture far away. They watched him from against the damp walls, looking through him with stony, iris-less eyes. One Mary was a young woman, her palms open to him, waiting to embrace him, her face so elegiac he sometimes came down just to look at her; he would stroke the rough edges of her eyelids, petting her like a stone cat. Her petrified lips were painted an obscene red, brighter than cherries, while the rest of her remained unpainted stone. Those lips centered his gaze, and one night he had kissed them, moving his tongue over the grainy surface. When he pulled away a cool breeze came down his back though the cellar door was closed; he turned around and saw no opening or crevice where the breeze could have come from. He did not kiss her again.

He dug and dug, pausing only to lift the tequila bottle to his lips and drink. The liquor spilled over his chin and down his ragged front. He took a spadeful of dirt and dumped it carefully over the head of one of the ceramic sheep; it settled there briefly, like a friar's wig, before disintegrating into falling grains. He laughed. He dug again and started to bury St. Joseph, who pleaded, from the waist up, arms outstretched, to bring down the forces of heaven, as if the very earth were slowly devouring him. The bottle of Cuervo was empty now, and he broke it against a leaning wall and held the jagged neck upright in the threadbare light; he wrote into the wall

> Sweetie pie, come down here to die,
> come down here to die,
> I will never leave you
> dry your eyes, dry your eyes

He stood back from his words to see how the stick-like letters looked on the wall and thought of Father O'Dowd and the priest's penchant for ripe strawberries dipped in whipped cream, how he dipped them one afternoon in the classroom he was sweeping. The letters looked like shards of glass, splinters from a broken vase, and Father O'Dowd's

2

voice came back to him, nervous, skittish, high-pitched: "Like them in cream, too, but don't tell Father Kastell." He had a comma of cream near his mouth; he used his left pinkie and licked it, smiling at Jesse.

He sat down Indian-style, throwing the bottleneck behind him. It made a tinkling sound against the soft earthen wall. On one side of him was the mound of freshly dug soil exhaling its long-held breath, like the breathing of a new world. He leaned against it, a natural pillow, and closed his eyes, resting there amid the pious stony faces, breathing in the cool dark humus like the private place between a woman's legs. They looked on as if they were waiting for him to change into one of them and join their eternal pity; even with his eyes closed he could imagine fissures beginning to form on their torsos and faces, small rivers that would break their bodies down, one delicate seam at a time. The dirt felt cool on his head, settling into his hair like smooth sludge or shit that would bury him whole. After a long interval, in which he heard only the sounds of his own drunken breathing and the rain beating against the cellar door, he got up and resumed his digging.

He thought of fireflies and the sea smell of a woman's clitoris and the way the soft flesh parted there like the innards of a fish dissolving into water and he thought of being chained to a dog kennel in the backyard as he howled with the hounds in the stink of newspapers that crackled like cool fire and the moon made blurry by summer mist and the taste of sugar at the peak of a snow cone stained with cherry flavoring and of his father beating his arms and legs with a mop handle behind the toolshed—and he thought of the myriad keys that dangled on his hip like broken stars, and all the rooms he locked and unlocked in the course of a day, and a septic tank by a river smelling of urine with long weeds growing around it, of its rusted belly and underside, and the vague apprehension of violence around the lake, and grasshoppers covered with white chalk pogoing away from his bare feet on a gravel road and disappearing into a desert of powdered rocks, and of his mother cooing softly with a drunk wetback and the knife he held to his chest in the closet as he watched the Mexican take his mother like a dog, and the little girl in his dreams who did not see him as he tried to break through the transparent screen that divided them and

Father Kastell, and the bronze chalice catching stained-glass sun, and the smell of pencil erasers and the small buds of girls' bodies and the half-opened tin of tuna he left at his table, the stone Marys a circle of frozen women who could not love him and the claw hammer he kept under his cot—all of these had led to his digging.

When he finally hit bone his wrist jolted back, sending a shiver up his arms and shoulders; it was bone on bone, hard, adamantine, his shovel the conductor between two abrupt surfaces that set his teeth on edge. He lowered himself into the small grave, got on all fours, and started to scoop out the clay with his hands. Slowly, tenderly he brushed away the dirt from a bone that seemed to grow in length and brightness with each brush of his hand, shining from out of the clay like the gleaming tooth of a prehistoric beast. The bone began to curve slightly, a delicate bow no fuller than the slant of iridescent light that sometimes came through the slatted blinds he cleaned in the schoolrooms.

He talked to the bone quietly, telling it that it was all right. The femur led to the shallow bowl of the pelvis, full-shape lines that pulled at his loins, and its cracked remains led to the bird-like rib cage that arched out of the dirt in sloping curves of blinding white. He visualized the stack of vertebrae he knew connected everything, his gentle brushing like the unearthing of a miniature city that led to the vision of all temples. He was straddling the bones now, a knee on each side so as not to crush their hollow shards, and as he brushed away at the dirt where he knew her face would be—if she had a face—he was no different than any lover at any time in the world who was brushing the hair away from the forehead of his beloved, a gesture so tender and tide-like in its graze that it could have been a breeze over the slow sweeping of grass that ran all the way to the horizon. His long hair dangled like strands of mud a few inches above the buried skull as he tried to see through the earth to the head he knew should be there. As he brushed and watched the first few specks of jaw begin to appear, he began to whimper and stammer and cry, moved by the picture of a face that had disintegrated long ago and the anguish that had led him to this place. Where the nose would be he imagined a copper ridge of freckles;

where the eyes, two pools of blue water dappled by sunlight; where the mouth, two perfect halves of a deep ripe fruit.

As he brushed away the dirt from the top of her forehead he discovered first the sweep of her long blond hair, unaffected by burial and decay; the more he dug, the more hair he discovered, until his heart began to hammer wildly in his chest as her hair took up the whole underearth of the cellar, extending like a flood of dark water unfurling in the pit. He jumped to the side and started to dig above the exposed bone of her head in a radius three feet away in a dirt halo; as he dug he discovered again the golden loom that shone out of the ground like wheat burnished by the sun. He scurried out of the grave agitated, and started digging a hole next to the one where she lay; he dug straight down, glancing up from time to time to see if the skeleton was still there, throwing the dirt over his shoulder.

The audience of stone virgins and saints grew taller as they leaned over the widening pit as if they would fall in. Soon he was panting and out of breath, working harder than before, a creature half-man and half-mud digging a small room of earth. Now he had two holes nearly equal in depth. He crawled out of the one hole to peer into the one where her hair began; he went back to his new hole and dug more carefully. When he thought they were nearly the same depth, he got on his hands and knees again and started scraping with the broken bottleneck. In a few moments he found the glistening chestnut hair and yelped out of fear and astonishment; there was no end to it, this river like bright water that undergirded the whole cellar in a subterranean current of thread; wherever he dug he found her long, golden hair disencumbered of earth.

He pulled her hair out of the ground like a man in a boat reeling in his lines. Her bones took on an incandescent brightness that shone up out of the earth; the amphitheater of stone watchers began to glow until everything in the cellar, hard and exposed, grew forth with light and he felt like he was pulling in more than bones, harvesting the meaning of years gone by and bodies who had known only outrage and pain. The stone figures, for so long enigmas to him that yielded only the futility of gestures frozen in time, began to relax their countenances

5

until he thought they might step forward or sag and crumple into dust. The river of hair did not abate. He gathered it around himself in a vast shawl, pulling and pulling, gathering in her reigns, when the rain stopped and he heard only the steady fabric of his reeling and a slow drip-drop somewhere above the stairs. When he reached the last of it he rolled it gently into one gigantic furl poised at the back of her broken skull like a grain stack; then he took off his belt and shirt and looped the belt around the shining hair and placed his shirt gently under the arc of her bones carefully, then slowly staggered to his feet.

Her bones were light in his arms as he stood in the grave, waist-high in contemplation and awe, the slow drip-drop above counting off the seconds and the minutes of his precious find. The stone figures took up space in the cellar like figures bent on keeping so still that the whole earth would stop turning, and with it the birds and the wind in the trees coming to rest like a great net over the branches. The cellar was no longer a dream chamber closing in all around him, but a new place of light coming up out of the ground. He spoke to the girl as the statues watched him:

> I know you came here after a lot of pain
> and I'm gonna take care of you.

The stone figures crept forward, tipping imperceptibly so that they moved downhill toward him, and the light in his eyes grew brighter until the cellar was no longer dank and dark but bright and dry like a white sail in the wind.

He stepped out of the grave he had dug and the stone figures tipped back in their places against the shining walls. He laid her carefully in a tarp he found in the cellar and started to ascend the damp stairs. It started raining again. At the top of the stairs he looked out of the smeared window that showed the streets misted over with fog and then he stepped out into the night, carrying the bones of the girl like the revelation of all his dreams.

George Garvin

I don't know what made me stop, but I did. You can't know about these things. I saw a truck and I pulled up ahead of it, about fifty yards or so off of I-80. Looked like he'd skidded off. I seen it before: car wrecks mostly, people walking around in a daze, holding a Kleenex up to the their nose. I once seen a woman holding her baby in a motel towel with "Double-Dealer" on the lace side of it, stolen from the place she was staying at, crying because she lost control and her station wagon slid off the road. But she was all right; they usually are, dazed and what-have-you, but still in one piece. I get calm when I see them; it don't bother me much until later, when I've had a few days to chew on it. Then it comes back like a bad dream and I'm right in the middle of it, asking questions nobody can answer.

I seen maybe eight, ten of these in forty-odd years of driving, most of them just scrapes and bad driving, but once in a while a few nasty ones where there's blood all over and they just lay there helpless and bleeding; one of them even died while I held her in my arms. The life just kinda drained from her eyes, like something falling down a dark dry well. I held her hand and watched her die—and I heard the wind in the aspens and a bird calling out. "Too late," I said to the paramedics, and then I spit on to the shoulder of the highway. I mean, what the hell else could I do? I didn't even know her. But I remember her eyes, and I remember what she said to me alone in the middle of nowhere: "I don't have any secrets to tell." And that was it. Then she died. So when I come up to this truck, I think to myself, *Hell, another poor son of a bitch pulling at my conscience.*

I had two days to make up because I had an axle problem down in New Mexico, and here I was slowing down for some jackass in a beat-up Chevy who skidded off for some goddamn reason. I had been driving twenty, thirty hours straight—I lost count somewhere near Leadville—and was dead tired, so sick of looking at my own red-rimmed eyes that sometimes I just closed my eyes. You do that sometimes. Defy the odds.

So I pulled up ahead, cranking it down and letting it idle. I looked out my side view to see if he was there. But all I saw in the reflection was his truck akimbo from the highway, and I thought, even as I was thinking it, *What the hell made me stop?* but before I finished thinking it, I got down from the cab and started to come over—and you know that feeling you get sometimes, when you start moving in a certain direction and nothing can make you stop, you feel pulled somehow—so I just kept walking toward the truck and called out "Anybody there? Anybody there?" with no answer, the engine still running. But something was wrong—anyone could see that straightaway. I kept going closer and when I got close enough I noticed a small wiggle in the back, like maybe there was something rocking back and forth there but gentle-like, 'cause you couldn't notice the rocking unless you were up close to it. And right then and there I should have turned heel, but did I? No, I didn't. And me, without so much as a pocketknife on me, walking toward the end of that goddamned truck, when I heard a small pitched moan or sigh, like an animal whining in its cage, and I got kinda still, I paused for a moment: it was either two teenagers fucking in the back or something else. I hoped it was fucking. But as I got closer I knew it wasn't no teenagers, and the rocking grew more steady, as if under the tarp something was building toward a climax.

Then I saw him: he come out of the woods buck naked and wild-eyed, carrying the longest goddamned knife I ever saw, the blade flashing in the sun, like some ghoul straight out of hell—and he had scars on his arms and a crucifix etched into his goddamned chest, and I thought, *What the fuck*, and if I was not a dead man I did not know it then, 'cause I ain't no sprinter at 260 with shit-kickers on, and he was hightailing it out of the woods like a goddamned ape, and even if I would've wanted to run I couldn't, and even if I could've said his name or appeased the crazed motherfucker, I was a dead man and a goddamned fool for stopping at all. And he run straight at me, past the rocking whatever-it-was in the back, and I thought *Holy shit, Holy shit*, and when he almost reached me he raised the knife in his hand and then I heard that moan turn into a song such as I have never heard, coming out of the flatbed like dawn colors, and we were eyeball to eyeball, but he wasn't looking at me anymore, just beyond me toward something only he could see.

It was singing, the sweetest, strangest singing, coming from the truck, like a hymn higher up than anything you have ever heard; it was high and fine, paper-light, so beautiful all you wanted to do was listen, come what may. I pissed myself. What a sight we must have been if only someone could've seen us: him naked and bleeding with that cross cut into his chest, me with a dark stain spreading across my crotch. Them bones sung for a long time, maybe it was forever, if forever exists, maybe it was outside of time and held us there before we were kids or after we died or even before we was a gleam in our daddy's eye, and after that singing I knew he wouldn't carve me up. Instead he looked straight into my eyes and cut his own skin just below his heart, like where they plunged the spear in after Jesus died.

I don't know what made me talk, but I did. I said I was sorry. I don't even know why. I said I forgive him. I said, "Please forgive me." I told him to be careful with his special freight. But nothing I said made any sense either to him or to me, pure gibberish. When whatever-it-was stopped singing, I just turned around and walked back to my rig. It was over, my old life was over. My boots made dull thuds on the hot cement. I sat in my seat a long time, beginning to get that damp, chilled feeling you get after some kind of upheaval. But I didn't move to clean myself up or get it in gear. I just set there. I put my head on the steering wheel and closed my eyes for a good long while. When I looked up again the truck was gone.

Mrs. Clyde J. Parker

Clyde, he was always one to poke gentle fun at me: he would say I was losing my mind or seeing things, maybe both. I seen this fella come up to the trailer park; I seen him turn around in that truck of his, like he was looking for something in our dirt cul-de-sac.

From the window I noticed the whites of his eyes, but they were unlike any I had ever seen. *Jesus, dear Lord, hear me pray now: that man is a stranger here to confiscate me.* I told Bounty to get down from the couch—"Git down now, Bounty," I said—but I've been saying that for ten years now and he ain't heard me yet. He's just a lap dog, my brother Elroy calls him, but he's a smart lap dog. He has ears like antennas. And who cares if he is a lap dog; he's a good dog, smarter than most people I know. Bounty was watching, too, and starting to growl deep inside his chest. Why we saw him together and at once, I will never know, like we were tuned in to the same radio station, both of us sensing something strange was gonna happen. The TV lost its picture then and became a weird blue light, and I just knew the stranger had something to do with it.

I pulled my curtain back to get a better view. Bounty stood on the back of the couch, shaking and barking. He got out of that truck with a knapsack slung around his shoulder, holding a tin cup with his free hand. *Well, what is this?* I said to myself. *What kind of mischief is he bringing home?*

And now I must digress, because it's part of what I saw and part of the story too, the story that never ends, the mystery of human beings. When Clyde said I was a weathercaster for human events he meant what I am about to tell you, that certain movements seem complete in and of themselves, contained, and my sweet velvet Jesus rocking on the back wall—whose eyes are clearer than the deepest blue lake or cornflower you ever saw—could tell you the same if your heart was clear and pure enough to hear it: that when it comes to human action and reaction the best way to react is to recognize your own small place as witness and therefore damner or sanctifier of a rite; that you do best by offering what you see up to God, so that it can come back in a form suitable both to him and to your feeble eyes. That's what Clyde meant when he said I could see through people. I let them do what they must rather than what I think they should.

I saw his heart beating in his chest. I saw it beating there, like a thing afire. But it was no normal heart. I let it wash through me, the knowledge, and I did not panic. I did not abandon faith at the moment of truth. He was either an angel or the Devil, maybe both, his long black hair stringy and uncombed, his beard ragged, his knapsack full of something lumpy and frail. His heart glowed. I watched him move from door to door, knocking and waiting. And each of my neighbors—good people, each and every one of them, if sometimes lost to the God who made them—opened their screen doors to a stranger and let him act out that part of the play God was author of, and soon to be more than witnesses, now part of the drama itself. He held out the cup. I saw what was in his mouth as he was saying words he did not really mean—or saying something only to test his listeners, like a musician who will tune up his violin to make sure it sounds right. He was asking for money, spare change, anything they could offer. I didn't ask, "What is this?" I didn't get indignant or put out, I knew his was a special er-rand. There was something about his idling truck that made me hopeful and afraid at the same time, like that truck was bewitched with a spirit not of this earth, covered with the colors of the land but a pale reflection of it, a kind of camouflage, like some duck that leaves the pond and the weeds from which it came. He was making his way down to me and Bounty; most folks just slammed their doors in his face. I knew what they thought: some bumpkin driving around, asking for change without even the excuse that he was collecting for some cause, just driving around and knocking on doors. Way past shiftless—reckless, more like, a kind of dare that went out from his eyes to see what you would do.

Would you give to him?

Would you find it in your heart to break down and help him? It did strike a body as funny-bone odd. It did seem out of nowhere, mysterious, full of hidden motives. And what did you plan to do about it, this sudden request for charity, a handout to a man who looked rough and wild enough to stuff a shirt with whiskey and lies? He had odd crisscrosses on his exposed arms, like maybe he fell in a patch of nettles or tried to swim his way through a barbed-wire fence. Well, now, this is new. But he did not take offense as the doors were shut on him; he did not try to plead with them or further denigrate himself in begging. Lord, he did not even seem to beg, just ask matter-of-fact, "Can you give me money?" Most folks, when proposed with such a thing, laugh outright or shout in your face. I knew what I would do. I knew it because it was already done, an accomplished thing, like I had been rehearsing all my life for this moment, going over and over it.

But the readiness cannot say what that moment will mean to you, and even if your heart is in your mouth—like mine was in mine—the moment, here at last, that you have waited for all your life, my life, here on this earth, even beyond the fifty years with Clyde and Apple and Jimmy and all their crises—Apple married too young to a man who did her no good, and Jimmy drifting from job to job and woman to woman, rootless—and now my lap dog Bounty who, Lord help me, has been the best company of all; even if you see the moment and recognize it for what it is, you still feel on the verge of dyin' or having a beautiful heartbreak, like God is gonna show you what he's gonna show you and your heart cannot bear it because you are human and not God and no one shall look on his face, amen. He was coming to collect me and I knew it.

When he knocked on my door I pulled my sweater tight around me, and Bounty, who usually sets up such a ruckus as you have never heard, didn't move at all and continued his steady growling. I opened the door. He stood a step down, right next to my pot of daisies, and his eyes were Jesus's eyes, just like those in my velvet portrait, and I said, in my best, clearest, strongest voice, "Come in," and he did. There was something about his knapsack slung over his shoulder that gave me pause, but I ain't one to pry. I knew every eye in that park was trained on my trailer, and if he should try to cause me harm they would all come a-runnin', with no small arsenal to fend him off with. I was calm as I could be in such a situation, but ended up talking mostly to myself.

"How can I hep you? I seen you turn around in our little drive, and I thought to myself, *This stranger is lost*, and though I am no great shakes at directions myself, you jus go right ahead and hep yourself to the phone book or the phone. You just hep yourself."

He did not move. He stared at me with black pillar eyes, and Bounty began to whimper instead of growl.

"I seen ya, son, asking for handouts: I will not ask why. I don't want the whys or wherefores. I need not. You're on a mission, ain't ya? And you come to collect me. Well, Jesus is my Savior—and he will protect me in this room, so if you are the Devil or an angel, I will not reveal it; nor will I reveal what I know of his will—which is much, because I am an instrument of his word—I will not reveal it. So go on, hep yourself to what you want or need, I know you're on a special errand from somewhere inside the earth, and me, just a sixty-six-year-old woman, I know what you come for, I know what you want even if I can't say it. I want you to be clean and I know it is not money you ask for, it is not anything anyone can give in terms of possessions, because I am possessed by the Lord—hep me, Jesus—and you know it and I know it." Then he took my face in his hands and moved it closer to his face, inspecting me, looking so deep into my eyes I was lost in the dark pits of space where there are no people, and we were locked up like that for maybe all of my life. Then he opened his mouth and inside was a spider dancing on his tongue, and I looked at it with fascination. The spider raised one leg like spiders do, like a question mark poised at the threshold of God's answer, and the spider moved down the long red furl of his tongue, and I opened my mouth then and the spider moved onto my tongue, and he said, he said, the only words he said to me,

"Swallow the dead girl"

and I did as I was told, I swallowed the spider that he said was a dead girl. And you know what? Know what? I swallowed a little girl, maybe ten or eleven, I swallowed her beautiful long blond hair and green eyes and limbs that were so precious they draped in my stomach like silk curtains. And I said, "Lord, so this is how you work," and she tasted fine and sweet, not like human flesh at all, if human she ever be, like sunflower seeds star-touched and pure. I swallowed the dead girl though I did not know her, and he planted a seed in me and I let it grow and my hair felt wavy and light, glowing all over; and in all my life, with all my dead behind and in front of me, the weeping, the tears, the lakes of my woe, I knew such a tenderness then that he gave me in the shape of a spider, and it was fine, fine, fine, surpassing the crude necessities of the earth and "mmm"—I said—"mmm," like Clyde touched me just once in our whole marriage, where his hands and tongue hit my deepest need, there, right there, the hovering spot in the center of all women, and I moaned like a knife passed through my heart. I felt lights flashing inside me, it was the girl who never became a woman in life becoming a woman inside me, so that I was two women, three, four, with their hungers and their hovering places, and we was all one woman. And he planted her there and it was beyond ruttin' and sex because I'm an old woman; it was so beyond all of that, you see, you just can't give it a name, like lightness or hearing waves coming closer, closer to sweep you away. All those tongues in my mouth were curving themselves around the same moans, and I shuddered like a decapitated snake and fell on the floor and writhed back and forth and said, "Caroline, Caroline," and we were one body, just one—and if you coulda seen him you would understand: that we are not meant long for this world, it is but a trial and tribulation, our real home is somewhere else, commencing the stars. I writhed, writhed, writhed—oh it was so nice and warm and lovely—I swallowed the spider and the dead girl.

You cannot know what it means to a woman my age to feel that way again, as if for the very first time. He planted his seed in me, yes. I lay ecstatic on my own floor—after two kids and Clyde and moving all the way from Florida when I was sixteen years old to be with a man I loved, yes, but who, after all, did not know finally what it was to treat his own woman. "Clyde," I'd say, if only he was here, "Clyde, you see how the inner parts of me work now, and you did not try to make me feel 'cause you was ignorant, and I forgive you. But you did not try."

And where are those oranges and pomegranates of my girlhood now? Where are they? I tell you they hang inside me and inside every woman, even inside the dead girl whose body I swallowed in the shape of a spider. I did not know then why the stranger came to give me this offering; before long, voices and people gathered outside and they worked hard to break the spell I was under, and it was many years till I came back to them, the stranger's eyes trained on me. "Why? Why? Why?" I asked through a veil of tears, but he did not answer.

"Louise, you all right in there?" Stella called from outside, and I could not answer. I got up onto my hands and knees and stretched like an alley cat. The stranger, who did bless me with coal black eyes, did so then again; he blessed me, Lord be praised, and I blessed him. I got up on my own accord and opened the door to let him out. "You let this kind stranger pass," I said, and there was Billy Ray standing a few feet away, not even trying to hide the sawed-off shotgun he held in his hands. The stranger parted them as I knew he would, a black bark boat going down a cold stream. Only later did I come to know the sorrow and violence of the dead girl's going, and then I got real sick and almost died. But that was later, when it was cold in the trailer and I felt the full tilt of my age. That was later, when he thought I could handle it. So that's why he gave me the ecstasy once't: to use it when it came to seeing clearly her death and the dry husks of my own hands. I do not walk now. Bounty does not bark at strangers anymore.

John Clearwater

I live in the rusted-out body of a Studebaker near a dry arroyo, a gigantic gutted fish you would love to catch then kill again, and cook my meals under the stars on a shovel I fashioned for cooking. The shovel is flat, okay, but dented in places, like dimples in a fat kid's face. I also use it to stamp the earth down inside my car, sand and dust being what they are out here, conditions you cannot hide from. I make my home in the sand.

My food cooks in the flat head of the shovel, so each meal I have is like others in shape, and sometimes I wonder how that is supposed to taste in my mouth, which is always the same and therefore comforting, like the food has no choice but to follow the landscape of the shovel. That's fine with me. I drape plastic sheeting and canvas over the top of the Stud—works fine—and if I want to see the stars I pull back the layers and see them. I don't let no woman or Indian come near my place. No biker or dope-smoking fiend, either. I can't drive the car, but I sit where I can look out across the land and if I see you first, you're dead. I have a pouch of ammunition I put under my pillow at night because you never know when you might need it; I like the smell and it makes me feel safe.

Why did I move out here? When I decided I couldn't take it anymore in society. When the TV went blinkety-blink-blink and I looked up at a billboard on a highway outside of El Paso that said

This Is God's Country
Don't
Drive Thru It Like
Hell

and I couldn't relate to what people were saying, thinking, doing around me, in everyday, commonplace life; when one day I found myself in a diner listening to the twang of country music and saw a deer's head with mangy fur and glassy-gloomed eyes mounted on the back wall looking deep into mine, like the void turned upside down, people around me talking about the Longhorns, farm prices, the goddamned government; when I thought, just for a moment, *Get out*, and the plea got lost somewhere between what I was thinking and what they were saying out loud and the click-clatter of silverware on ceramic plates. It was all a ceaseless noise to me and my wires got crossed. I don't blame no one in particular. I miss Jo-Jo, the red-haired waitress who made my coffee just right, with a pencil behind her ear. And Earl, the fat, good-natured slob who pretended to run the place from the back of the kitchen, though it was Jo-Jo's show all the way.

I'm not saying there aren't good people, I'm not saying that. But when what was coming out of most people's mouths—outside that beloved diner—where you know the great minds of the country congregated and planned futures, overthrows, revolutions, dikes, and were so much sawdust and nonsense—useless as communication and birdshit for brains—when that was the climate and not just a passing storm, and I saw blue-haired teenagers with baby pins in their noses, and worse, *worse*, people driving to work in the a.m. with nothing going on in their eyes, mouths moving soundlessly into cell phones—I couldn't take it, couldn't take it and I don't even know why.

One day I found myself in a mall and I saw the vast array of people in the food court stuffing themselves with jalapeños, egg rolls, and ice cream, strings of gaudy blinking lights hung from the rafters saying "Look at me, Look at me," and palm trees, artificial palm trees swathed in pink ribbons with a vaulted, funnel-shaped glass roof letting in some kind of artificial light but where it actually came from I have no goddamn idea. *What is this?* I thought. And music, piped-in synthesized madness, and candy wrappers lying on the ground with more mystery and soul than the hands that discarded them, and giant beetle-shaped wheelchairs for the elderly and strollers for infants.

What are people supposed to do in that kind of fucking rodeo? What are they supposed to be? You tell me. You tell me. You can't even *read* there, for chrissakes, let alone be a real person with a beating heart and eyes that switch back and forth. You can't believe that anything else is real because you're not real. If you were real, why the hell would you be there in the first place? It's no place to be, no place. *Que pasa aqui.*

I got the shakes and the shivers and the jim-jams, and I got the hell out. But not before I had a regular meltdown. My wife left me for harboring revolutionary ideas: "You don't ever go out and you're bitter and I want to have some fun." Bitter? Fun? What the hell did that have to do with anything? That's the exact center of nowhere, and you're in it, lady. You're circling the drain of your own futility, so have affairs, have affairs. Whoever fucks you is the Devil, and I can't do it anymore.

Evelyn took off with a man ten years younger with bleached hair and earrings; now they watch TV and suck on the stale ice cubes of each other. And I know why she left me, which had nothing to do with flowering bitterness or any other kind of weed: because, goddammit, I was onto something and she couldn't take it, and the yellowed clippings of different articles (I was weaving a tapestry around the symptoms of this country's demise before it fell into the shitter) started to feel like tobacco leaves in a South Carolina hut, and too much, too much, I came to know too much and it drove her out. But to say I don't think of her is a lie, and dog food is all right if you're really hungry, and I pray like a snake worshipping the sun because it's no time to be anywhere you cannot be without losing your mind. No time.

I sold my truck, my furniture, gave away or ripped up most of my clothes, and got blind drunk for two weeks straight. The days were packed together like a deck of playing cards until each one no longer had a name or anything else to call it, just a nondescript pack that went higgledy-piggledy into some kind of sucking vacuum where you could not touch or smell the world; and my view, if it is a view, is that if you cannot feel something setting up a tent or a chorus in your soul, then you are not alive. Comprendo? Otherwise what? You let them control you. And *them* is more than your two-bit job punching computer keys all day, or driving your bed-sized Toyota to a job that nibbles away at your life. It's everything around you that lies, lies, lies, like a giant tele-screen flashing images all day of a game-show host with perfect teeth whose face is half-preserved in formaldehyde, reconstructed from the chin up and whatnot, okay, telling you to buy this or to be that and to not miss this or for sure miss that. It's just so much bullshit. And when that day or hour awakens you, and you quit your job as the night watchman of a power plant then *look out*: you'll get very drunk and belligerent, land yourself in the clinker, and dream of blowing the whole fucking thing up. But I'm not no bomb-maker, not anymore, anyway, because even if I did blow a mall sky high, what good would it do when they're already starting in on a new one right next door?

I stay out here instead and eat sand like a crab. I canvas the area for aluminum cans on my bicycle (don't call it a goddamn bike)—a twenty-some-mile radius that is flat and agreeable to my legs—and if it gets too hot then I lie still in the shade of a tree or building and watch the clouds pass by like a Hopi medicine man. I smoke when I got 'em. The clank of my flattened cans is my version of wind chimes, and what is nice about it is my bicycle controls the tempo. And people, what can I say about people? I'm no misanthrope, though I hate to see another face around my camp, okay, because this is where I live and do my work. Sometimes at dusk I pedal to the top of a flat red plateau and gaze into the valley below where the city lights shimmer in the dying heat, like white embers that are slowly heating up when they should be cooling down.

And I think of them in their apartments and houses and watch the blinking lights of airplanes coming in from the east and the people's drooping eyes before they go to sleep and their tired backs and feet, and I wonder what they are thinking, what sorrows are they enduring or what tiredness, what small joys, with probably a piece of lint on a kid's head somewhere. Because I have lived their life in my own small way and it is not life but the bankrupt equivalent of the walking dead moaning in their death-wraps. Wake up, you fuckers! (but I don't say it—I breathe it softly, like a prayer). It is a holy and heartbreaking sight, but only at night, when the city does not know it is being watched and all those people are unaware that their lives are tragic and small and fading into the atmosphere after three straight hours of sitcoms.

And solitude, sweet solitude, where the face of God is everything you see, and your inner ear strums with the silence or with the call of meadowlarks: this is the life I am supposed to live because I am living it. And we are all alone anyway, it just takes you a long time to learn it if you are surrounded by other people. I will say this: I will say this: wherever I am going or have been is not for me to know. And wherever I end up is preordained, with a windmill and slats all its own, turning clockwise in a pattern you can follow until it becomes a shaded bruise through which to view the sun. Your life is a color, just a color, that's all, and who can stop it, then, from being what it needs to be, what it already is because that's the way it's supposed to be? Then you know you have arrived without going anywhere at all. It's a quiet, good life out in the desert; I am so used to its silence and small cursive writing on the dunes around my car, it's like a great big tear running through the middle of my chest—the immense distance of the desert slowly filling me up—until I know eventually I'll be ripped wide open and then maybe I won't even need the occasional whore now and then. My ultimate goal is to turn into a rock and follow the riverbeds to the ocean, where I'll be turned into pearly white sand.

My name is John Clearwater, and I'll tell you what I saw if you're quiet and listen real hard. But only if you're quiet.

Are you listening? Are you awake? Are you listening?

I saw them come on through the windshield of my shelter that's no windshield at all but torn plastic sheeting I pull back to view the immensity of the sky. Holy delirium, but it wasn't no mirage. It was them, I saw that it was them, walking across the desert in shimmering heat waves a few miles away, him carrying the dead girl in his arms before she turned up as a heap of bones and disintegrated into dust. I began to eat the sand around me, picked it up by the handful to fill my quaking mouth.

They come out of nowhere, but I saw they were as old as the world and just as sorrowful, someone, somewhere, everywhere at once carrying the body of a dead girl for all time from one place to another, the girl slain on the altar of some injustice that will never be solved in this here abandoned world, lashed by the elements until they was the only journey there was, just him and that girl with me betwixt them and the God of everlasting love. Rocked back and forth on my hams, bit my lower lip until it bled to taste that bitter iron, and started keening along with them in the great cataclysmic fallout. Had to be that way, though no one can say why. Wasn't no crime that could be solved, her murder just the thing that fed that great inferno in the sky. Maybe he was taking her back to the basement of that church in Nebraska before she became the bones and he dug her out—I don't know—but he was out there in the desert after she was killed and I saw 'em, I saw 'em come on and my whole wasted life was a testament to that seeing, the one thing I was meant to do after I became that wandering travesty of the hobo towns and rest stops.

He sewed the earth with his footsteps because he had it to do, take that dead girl on the road and show her to people who needed to see her, who *had* to see her like some great salve come to blast them out of their fucking stupor. They were coming on, coming to get me, and this was what I'd be waiting for my whole life and didn't even know it till then, fool that I was and am. Just sun and wind, red rim rocks, and forever, the music of the whited-out stars playing inside my head. *John, I said to myself, all has been a prelude to this: the waste of your life is but a preparation and a reparation, and as you taste the sand and the dust whistles through your nostrils you are alive, my son, so here you are.*

And I whispered to him across that desolate and parched land: "Come inside my circle, boy, come inside my circle."

Son. Son. Sit here.

I, John Clearwater, who have been moving in the bowels of this great country for years now, on the fringe of its great sleeve, have seen omens in abandoned shopping carts, in encounters with crows, wheel rims left on the side of the highway, credit card receipts blowing into ditches: this is why I came out here, because I am a man and I still cling to falsehoods. Still, I see now (the seeing was given to me) that unless we change *now* we will die. Unless you take this difficult path—the path that leads nowhere because it is everything you are not, shorn of all possessions—then whatever I would say or will say is ceaseless noise spinning its spokes in space and shining in the spinning. Then you cannot help yourself. You are on loan from God. You cannot seek other than the truth. Then they are almost here. Then they are upon you.

Are you ready for them?
Are you ready?

Easter Hollins

Day of my sixteenth birthday, years ago, Easter weekend. That's my name. Easter. Easter Hollins. Folding chairs and tables set out in the backyard. Lots of nice white linen tablecloths, like sailboats on green water, ready to blow away in the wind. But Mom has anchored them down with glass bowls of water, with flower petals floating inside them. So it's just the ends of the tablecloths rippling in the breeze, just the very ends.

Dad wandering around with a glass of white wine in his hand, looking a little lost in his own backyard. Strange but sweet, mostly sweet. I'm sixteen years old going on twenty-one, something like that. Tall for my age, or any age. What's the word? Well-developed. Taller than a lot of boys. Gangly, Dad called it. All knees and elbows sticking out at awkward angles. One of my friends even calls me Scissors.

All the tables set up, but some of them at a slight downward angle, very slight, on the electric green grass. Lightning makes the grass greener. Did you know that? There was some lightning the night before. You don't see grass like that too often—maybe in the tropics or some place like that. Dad took care of it like it was his own skin—or my skin. Tenderly, you know. Like he really wanted to take care of it.

They're all coming over and I'm embarrassed, I really am, because some of these people I don't even know. Coming to celebrate my sixteenth birthday, because I'm the firstborn. The party wasn't my idea. Mom made such a big deal of it, way out of proportion if you ask me, but I don't want to hurt Mom and Dad's feelings. They're excited for me. And my name is Easter. So the two coincide. Chip's sulking around, he's mad that I'm getting all the attention, but it wasn't my idea. I kept trying to tell him that.

Dad looks lost walking around the yard, with that glass of wine in his hand. He always looks lost to me, or maybe a little confused, like he just landed here from some other planet. Mom used to call him Space Man. He didn't take it personally. Has a really good sense of humor. I don't know why they're so excited, excited for *me*, since up to that point all I did was get born. That's not such an accomplishment, right? Happens every day. Dad saying, "There can only be one firstborn." Mom holding back the tears. Made me feel special and embarrassed at the same time. Maybe a little proud. Just a little, though I don't even know why.

I can wear all of Mom's clothes, but not her shoes because they're too small. Even had older guys, men even, hit on me, if you can believe that. Easter was always my favorite holiday, not just because of my name. Seemed to me that every other holiday was about dying in a way, you know, falling leaves for Thanksgiving, snow on Christmas Eve even if it is Jesus' birthday. Even Halloween's about ghosts and goblins, monsters. But Easter. Easter. That's about new life, springtime, things coming up out of the ground. Flowers and birds coming back. Jesus again, this time for real.

We don't want for anything, a real nice upbringing, our own rooms, nice clothes, nice house out in the suburbs. Not like some kid living in rubble somewhere, South America or a bombed-out city in the Middle East. The differences used to bother me, they really did. I thought they were important somehow. I looked around. I could see it with my own eyes. The haves and the have-nots. We were definitely on the side of the haves. All my family's friends were haves too. Parents were doctors or lawyers. Swimming pools. Jacuzzis. Trips to Hawaii and Cancun. Like it was expected. No big deal. Normal. In the order of things.

But the have-nots, that was a different story. I don't just mean the news on TV, which just presents a flat picture, no real life there, at least for me. Everyone knows that. But at school. You know, the poor kids—or at least poorer, because where I'm from everyone is pretty much the same. There were a few, though, the families just getting by. And my heart went out to them. As lame as that sounds. I mean, it's so easy to say that, but to really mean it, to really feel it in your bones ... that's something else entirely.

It was a perfect day for a birthday. No one could ask for more. A little wind, like I said. But the wind made it exciting too, added some urgency to the whole thing. If you didn't know better and just stumbled into it, you'd think it was this chic party for grownups or something. But I was just a kid, even though the party's for me. I felt kinda absent from it, like all this stuff and festivities were swirling around me but they weren't really *touching* me.

In addition to a few of my friends there were lots of grownups there, really well dressed, wearing the kinds of clothes you'd imagine people would wear on the first really nice day of spring. Everyone in bright, sun-washed colors, light clothing. Kinda intimidating. Whether Mom meant to do this or not, I felt like I had to entertain each one, make sure they had a good time. I felt a duty to personally thank each person, spend some time with them. It was stressful and a lot of work.

Dad would wander to the edge of our lush yard and stare off into space, or look like he was listening for something but couldn't quite figure out what it was, something more real than what was at his back, his first daughter's over-the-top birthday party and everything that went along with it. I really thought I understood him at that moment, like he was a separate person, with his own thoughts and feelings that had nothing to do with me.

No one could say he wasn't smart, that's for sure. First one in his family to go to college and all that. His brother—Uncle Nate—was a janitor before he died. And he'd lost most of his teeth. Nothing but gums. But Dad always insisted that Uncle Nate was a lot smarter than he was. He only visited us once, when I was about ten. He drove all night to get here, like twelve hours or something. He and Dad had beers on the porch under the stars. I could hear them talking in low tones long after midnight. I didn't care what they were saying so much as the quality of their voices. Isn't that strange? Listening to them talk like that was one of the most peaceful sounds I ever heard.

Dad's the vice president at a plastics company called Recon. Eventually he even came to own a part of it. They make all kinds of things, car seats and stuff like that. The plant's located in this run-down part of town, a lot of empty warehouses, train tracks, and weeds, graffiti. It was the kind of place you'd imagine hell was like, almost an exact copy. In my mind it's always cloudy above the plant as it spews forth this stench from a giant chimney. Terrible. Chip and I worked there in the summer two, three years. I was in the office and he was down on the floor.

Dad wanted us to see what it was like so we would never have to work those awful jobs. He'd say to us in his real quiet voice, "You don't want to do this for the rest of your life. That's why you're down here. So you'll remember it." And I never asked him the question that's been on my mind ever since, which is, "Then why do *they* have to work here?" because I knew he didn't have an answer. No one does.

Driving home from the plant was like entering a different world. It was hard to imagine two such different places existing side by side. But apparently this happens all the time. Some people have to live in the world of the plant and do that kind of work and others don't. Like Uncle Nate. And you don't want to be one of those people who have to work that kind of job. That's how it was explained to me without anyone really saying it out loud, out of politeness or embarrassment or something. Mom and Dad didn't need to. We saw it all around. But it bothered me, it really did. The question was always *why*. *Why* did it have to be that way? *Why*? No one could ever give me a satisfactory answer to that question. Maybe no one ever will.

Mom always had a flair for throwing parties, for entertaining people. She was like Martha Stewart before she got thrown in jail. Mom was a typical housewife, I guess you'd say, but she took her work very seriously. She was always volunteering at the hospital or the church or baking someone muffins because someone was sick or a relative had died.

The neighborhood where we lived was really nice, clean and every-thing, but the houses were all pretty much the same. Two- or three-car garages, that kind of thing. Winding driveways. Sculpted bushes. Even the neighbors seemed the same, with some minor differences. I remember walking across someone's well-tended yard thinking, *You could hit a golf ball at every single one of these houses and no one would blame you because they looked like the kind of houses that were hit by golf balls all the time, so why the fuss?* It's just great to live next to a golf course or *on* a golf course, and that's just the price you pay and almost a badge of honor, too. They have insurance for that kind of thing. It was a privilege to be hit by a golf ball because it's kind of a status sym-bol. So go ahead and whack away. The sound of breaking windows will never be more cheerful.

When someone goes away all of a sudden and doesn't come back, the people who are left behind feel cheated, betrayed. They even get a little angry, even if it isn't your fault. They look around with wounded eyes. It's not that they blame you, don't get me wrong, it's just . . . they can't help not expecting some kind of reward for their suffering. It never occurs to them in a million years that their suffering *is* their reward. And even if you do go back, even if you *could* go back, they want to see you as you used to be. They don't want to see you changed because they've been through enough already. So it's almost like two fears—the fear that you're never coming back and the fear that you will. And the added fear that there's nothing they can do about it one way or another, and disappearing and reappearing won't help them.

The party began at one o'clock sharp. Mom was a stickler for punc-tuality. The cream-colored cars started parking on the street, and I was expected to greet and say hello to each person. The Maxwells arrived first, none of this fashionably late thing. They were my parents' oldest friends and I was in the same grade as their daughter Sara. Sara and I got along fine, but it was always like we were competing for something that didn't have a name. I had no idea what it was. She used to do this weird thing with her hands when I first knew her, some kind of gesture, like an unconscious tick. People started to make fun of her and she had a hard time quitting.

Then a group of old ladies arrived from church. They did volunteer stuff with Mom. Mrs. Barber, Mrs. Howe, Mrs. Clarkson, Mrs. Stevens, all there, mostly widows, smiling and holding onto each other's arms. They came in in this slow-moving procession, their hair all white, like a slow-moving almost radiant cloud, and people just parted in front of them, magically stepping out of their way. I never realized old women could be powerful that way. They looked like this tiny group of what? Holocaust survivors or something, and people let them pass and then closed around them. But the strange thing was these four women all holding onto each other, hanging on for dear life, moving like turtles, and then I heard it—this real faint and far-off siren, this distant wail— and it was like their bright white hair was blessing the siren and the yard and every person in it. Probably some guy in an ambulance after a heart attack, maybe about to die, but with them walking in their slow-moving march the siren didn't sound so bad. Serious and life-threatening, but not bad. In fact, it almost sounded like a song of . . . praise. I could picture the tubes hooked up to the dying patient and this young, really good-looking medic sitting hunched over, right next to him in the ambulance, and it was like, well, it was just very moving and very clear. To me it was clear. To me it was like . . . deliverance.

It seemed like Mom had invited everyone. She was very democratic that way. After an hour people were still coming, and they stacked their presents on this special table, and I doubt very much that any other sixteen-year-old ever had so many presents. I knew for a fact that Chip was mad at me. He finally came out of the bathroom and he walked past me with his shirt sticking out and he never said a word or even looked in my direction. What was that all about?

Dad used to say all the time, "No one is going to die of starvation around here." He would just say this out of the blue. We'd be in the basement or watching TV, or eating quietly at the dinner table and he'd just suddenly say out of nowhere, "At least no one's going to die of starvation here." Or on family trips we'd be driving along, each one lost in their own thoughts, and he would just boom out in this uncharacteristic voice, "At least none of us is going to starve!"

I mean, why did he have to say that so much? What was he trying to prove? It was strange and absurd when you really thought about it, because here we were, this well-off family, and Dad would just almost cry out, "At least no one's going to starve!" Starve? What did he mean by that? Mom went grocery shopping every Thursday and came home with a boatload of food. Chip alone drank like two gallons of milk a week.

Maybe Dad said that all the time because he grew up poor and used to have chickens scratching in the backyard. Just one or two chickens they kept around until, well, you know, until they ran out of everything else to eat. Then naturally they ate the chickens. But I also thought that Dad was saying that for a reason, maybe even a subconscious one. He was trying to explain something to himself and to us as well. He was right—we weren't about to starve. But the way he said it was kind of sorrowful, like he was talking about a personal wound or something.

I knew some girls in school who had bulimia and anorexia, and some even said that I was one because I was always so skinny. But believe me, I ate as much as I could handle. Then it hit me one day and really made me stop and think. We were coming back from somewhere as a family, we all had just gone to church, and as we were getting out of the car Dad said it again to no one in particular, "At least no one's going to starve around here!" I think he said it as a delayed response to Mom's question about dinner that night or something. But I suddenly felt the pain and deep misery behind Dad's offhand comments about not starving and it, like, bloodied my whole body. Starving? I don't know if I had ever been hungry, really, really hungry beyond the usual daily cycle of things, let alone starving. I literally had no clue about what Dad was talking about.

I thought, *I have to understand what Dad's saying in my own way. I just have to take one tiny step in that direction.* So I didn't eat dinner that night. Mom said, "Aren't you going to eat anything?" And I said, "My stomach doesn't feel right." She was worried, she was concerned for a moment, but the moment passed. And I could watch the rest of my family eating, drinking their drinks and asking for the salt and pepper. It was like watching this slow, agonizing dance where you just know at the end of it that someone has to die. That's what I kept thinking, for some reason. How long could someone go without food? I had heard a very long time. But I never knew a single person who had ever come close to starving, not a single one. So I went to bed that night without dinner and I went the whole next day without food, too. When I thought about eating my heart started to beat very fast, like it was about to jump out of my chest. In the morning I told Mom I was late for school and would eat something there, and she must have been unusually preoccupied or something because it wasn't a problem.

I had gone twenty-four hours without food for the first time in my life and I have to say that things started to look a little different. At some moments in the day the thought of eating made me nauseous and at other times that's all I wanted to do. I knew I would have to eat something at dinner or Mom would get suspicious. But, you know, I didn't really want to. So that night I broke my fast and ate with the family. But it was like a delicate string snapped inside of me that was just starting to grow. I heard it snap and fall away into dark empty space. At least I knew what it was like to go one day without food. To me it was very humbling and intense, like so much of my life had been lived in terrible excess. And whenever Dad said, "At least no one's going to starve around here!" I honestly felt like he was grieving or making fun of himself, or admitting in a weird way that he had betrayed himself or us in some way.

Back to the party. All in all, apart from my reluctance, I'd have to say that things started to look different right in front of my eyes. People kept showing up and it seemed like the party was important to them somehow, so maybe I'd been wrong. I had very recently learned about all kinds of sex from a crude book a friend had showed me and I wondered in an idle but curious way how many people had had sex before the party and how many would after. Maybe half, seventy-five percent? Maybe even during, if they could slip away somehow.

Mom had set up three buffet tables loaded down with food and even an ice sculpture of a swan. You know how it is at a party like that: people trying not to stuff themselves, but they keep refilling their plates because the plates are so small. The ice sculpture alone was as big as a small child. And even though it was a swan it looked more like a hawk or eagle, really ferocious. I sat and ate at the head table. That's what Mom called it anyway, the head table, like the tables formed a body. It had wreathes of flowers draped on the sides to set it off from the other tables.

The whole arrangement spoke of something that in no way could be refuted: This is how you throw a party for your teenage daughter if you have the money and the determination to pull it off. Yes. There is no other way. It wasn't, like, flaunting it, but it was very close. Awfully close. Mom would never admit or even understand what I mean when I say it, but her taste was always a little violent. The way she threw parties was the way a general might organize a battle or the overthrow of a country. She had the objective clearly in mind and saw all the obstacles between her and it and, well, she got rid of them one by one, that's what she did. Systematically. Without batting an eye.

I was sitting at the table with Mom, Dad, Chip, and the Maxwells. Everyone was talking except me. I guess I had nothing to say. The food was delicious but for some reason I wasn't hungry. I knew what was coming. Mom was going to ask people to give speeches. She would make them talk about me. They'd have to stand up and clink their glasses with their teaspoons and knives and clear their throats. "I have something to say," one of them would offer. And what had I done to deserve any of it? Nothing. All I had done was grow another year older. So I sat there as the speeches started, cringing in my seat, Mom's red lipstick like the blood of a clown, and I started to have all these strange thoughts.

I thought of how violent a birthday party could be. Not fistfights or bombs going off, just this awful and forced way of doing things and expectations that everyone had to behave and even say almost the exact same things. That we were perfect or almost, that our lifestyle was preordained, something even the gods would envy, that we deserved everything we had and it just couldn't be any other way. It couldn't have been stranger than if I had been sitting there naked, waiting to be thrown into a volcano. I wanted to be happy but there was this strange knowledge pulling at me, gnawing inside of me, that something about this whole setup wasn't quite right, even if I couldn't put it into words. Apparently this happens all the time. You'd never see a cripple or a homeless person at a party like that. Maybe a secret drug addict or two, but not the kind you'd see on the streets. You'd never see a religious fanatic, a desperate artist, or an eccentric lover of animals. No. You just wouldn't see them. But you knew they existed. You knew they were around somewhere, like rumors of a distant planet.

To say that people can live however they want . . . that they are really free to choose . . . well, I just don't believe that. I just don't see much evidence of it at all. In the park inside our neighborhood we also had these artificial and manmade hills. I can't tell you what these hills did to me. I had this like . . . cosmic reaction. We played on these artificial hills and we watched the sun go down over them. They were roughly the size of sod houses, some even bigger. I didn't believe in the reality of these hills at all. They were there my whole childhood, and I had the same reaction almost every time I saw them or walked over them. A part of me, just a small, precious part, didn't want to be alive. Now, you might say that's a strange reaction, an odd kind of dramatic response, but someone, some landscaper, had to design these particular hills and the foliage around them. And someone else, an entire community of people, had to approve them, agree to put them in a particular spot. A whole variety of factors had to be weighed and considered. And that's what filled me with such despair and disbelief—that so many people actually preferred artificial hills to the natural landscape.

Where do you even begin to talk about something like that? I remember one evening, I went up to Dad while he was out on the porch looking into the distance, and I asked him, "Dad, you know those hills in the park? They're not even real." And the way he looked at me, the way it registered: "I know it," he said quietly. "Some things just don't make much sense, do they?" But they did to me. Or, rather, I felt them. Or, rather, their injustice went through me, like a cold wind on its way to the ends of the earth.

Why couldn't I be happy with the party? Why couldn't I accept it?

My name is Easter. It was the beginning of spring. Everyone wore vibrant or pastel colors, everyone was talking, and the air was soft and fragrant, the kind of early spring day that the poets write about. The speeches were sincere or gently teasing; people said nice things and improvised on the spot. No one seemed too upset, or they kept their private grief buried deep inside them; they put up a brave front and for many of them it was no front at all.

I walked away.

I saw my opportunity and I took it, without telling anyone. Slipped away from my own birthday party like an invisible theft where I was stealing from myself, didn't tell anyone where I was going. Could have made up some excuse: wanted to exercise my long legs, wanted to see the green coming up, listen to the birds, have boys yell at me from their car windows. But . . . nothing. I gave no notice of leaving. Maybe twenty, thirty minutes would pass, and then Mom would ask someone, "Where's Easter? Have you seen Easter?" I didn't leave to be mean or spiteful. I didn't go to hurt anyone's feelings. The speeches had been given, everyone had had their say, the cake went into the mouths of the old, the young, the middle-aged, people with canker sores from all kinds of stress, every step of the party had been executed. No one could say I hadn't done my duty or carried out my responsibilities.

I left through the open garage into this growing rectangle of sunlight, down the long slope of the driveway, and I didn't look back, not even once. The appalling artificial hills were in front of me, but I walked away from them. By this time Chip was back in the bathroom. My brother masturbating in a clean linoleum bathroom with all these well-dressed guests milling about downstairs—this remains to me the best description of how and where we lived, better than anything else I can think of. I was walking fast, but I didn't feel out of breath, I didn't feel anxious that I would be caught. And what kind of betrayal was this, exactly? I didn't think of it in those terms. The party would go on just fine by itself, like a kid's top spinning on the ground. I thought I understood perfectly why God would create a world and then just walk away from it, let it carry on by itself, until someone finally asked, "Where did God go? Has anyone seen him?"

As I walked away from the party and the noise grew less and less, I felt this kind of release, almost sadness, like I had just witnessed some kind of upheaval. It wasn't so hard to leave after all. I walked five blocks, six before I even turned to look back. But no one was there. They probably wouldn't have wanted to go where I was going, though I didn't know where that was. I looked around and saw the big familiar houses where two or three families could have lived, and I saw them with fresh eyes. They looked . . . uninhabited, like no one lived there. As if a toxic cloud had come and killed everyone, leaving the houses intact. I didn't see a single face. Only two cars passed me on my walk and they slowed down and then sped up again. Some guy yelled out his window, like I knew he would.

I felt like an explorer of some unknown territory, walking across a landscape she had seen before but only in her dreams. No food, no backpack, no weapons. Only herself. I walked roughly two miles in the same direction, west. Even if I had wanted to I couldn't just rush back to the party. It took me a half hour to get that far, so it would be at least another half hour home. By that time I thought my absence would be felt. Mom would be looking for me, Dad would be enlisted in the search, even Chip—all of them would be asked where I was. "Have you seen Easter? Did she tell anyone where she was going?" No, it wasn't fair to do that to Mom. But I didn't think it was fair to stay there either. Even though it was spring, I remember wishing I had brought a light sweater because the day was wearing on. I just told myself to keep going. So I did.

And then I saw him.

This older guy with long hair sitting in a park. He was at least as old as my math teacher, probably older. His black hair was practically longer than mine. But there was something about him, even from a distance, that drew me toward him, that made me want to know him better. I almost had the feeling he had been waiting for me, but that was impossible. At first we casually noticed each other and then we openly stared. He was about fifty feet away, sitting on a park bench. I felt that I had come to the end of my brief journey, that I wouldn't be able to take another step until he said something. Maybe it was time to get back to the party, but I didn't really think so. So we kept staring at each other awhile. And then he said to me, he asked me one question that would change my life forever: "Would you like to go for a drive?"

And I said yes.

I could have stayed away from him. There was no reason for me to get into a strange guy's car, especially on my birthday on a beautiful spring day. I could have kept on walking. I would have on another day, at another time, if something had lured me away. But I didn't. Why did I go with him? Why did I give up so much by getting into a stranger's car? Why didn't anyone see us? How could I just leave like that, on my own birthday even? I could have easily turned my back on him. So why? I made the choice to leave my birthday party where I was deeply loved, where I had everything, and chose to walk away without a word to anyone. He didn't force me into his car. I went voluntarily. You couldn't say I had been kidnapped. The idea of that is laughable. I . . . wanted to go. I was waiting to go, to be asked by someone to just go away. To leave. But who or what is truly responsible for my leaving? Was it the artificial hills in the park across the street or Mom's lipstick or Dad's starched collars before he went off to work? Our perfect, well-ordered life in West Omaha? What was it, precisely, that made me leave and made me want to leave? What was it? And why? Why? Why?

We drove into the sunset in his beat-up pickup truck and he bought me an ice cream cone on the way, though I wasn't really hungry. But I ate it anyway. The farther we went the easier it became. I *couldn't* go back then. I didn't want to. I had passed an invisible boundary and was just waiting to see what would happen next.

So later, hours later, when we had finally made it to this motel way out in the country, he said he wanted to show me something and I got a little scared. The reality of what I had done was starting to sink in. He said I reminded him of a girl and I said, "What girl?" But he didn't answer me. We walked into his room and there was something wrapped up in the corner in all these blankets. He said she was under the blankets. "Do you want to see her?" he asked, and, without thinking about it, I nodded. Then he took the blankets off and I saw her.

She had all the colors of the world coming off her mutilated body, and they were brighter than any rainbow. A sound was coming out of her too, a high-up, eerie sound unlike any I had ever heard. I think she was trying to talk to me, but light was pouring out of her mouth instead of words and I passed out right there on the floor.

I stayed with them for about twelve days. Later he told me she wanted a girl around her age to talk to, but we didn't talk. He said she appreciated the way I listened to her. He dropped me off at a gas station three miles from my house. He made sure no one was looking, and then he told me firmly but politely to get out of the truck. I never did learn his last name until I read about it in the paper. Then he drove away. A week and a half after I left my birthday party I walked back home wearing some gym clothes he had bought for me. My gray dress and red heels were in a duffel bag.

I didn't feel like damaged goods. I didn't feel humiliated at all. I pulled my hooded sweatshirt over my head so no one could see me. Walking home was the hardest, longest thing I ever had to do. When I walked up our familiar street and saw the artificial hills a chill passed through me, like a blade of ice cutting up my spine. But there was little I could do about it. The house didn't look any different. On the outside nothing had changed. I walked through the open garage and into the basement. The door was unlocked. I stood in the basement and heard Mom pacing upstairs. All the pain and suffering I had caused her, all the worry. I felt like a ghost in my own house until I remembered that I really didn't feel at home there. Or anywhere, for that matter.

Everything was different because *I* was different. I walked away from all that affluence and love, had turned my back on it. It was either the most hurtful thing ever or the most glorious. Maybe even both. Nothing could undo the damage I had done or what I had put my parents through. And if I had to do the same thing over again, if I had the same small window of opportunity to just walk away, I realized then and there that I would have done it. In a heartbeat. Because I had to, in order to see her. And I could never tell them why. When I came upstairs Dad was sitting in his chair with the paper on his lap, staring out the window. Mom was pacing the kitchen. I didn't know where Chip was. Dad looked older than I had ever seen him, and shrunken somehow.

"I'm home, Dad," I said, and it took him a second to recognize me. Mom came screaming out of the kitchen, sobbing and clawing at me like a drowning woman. Dad came over, too, and we huddled in the center of the room, just the three of us, grasping at each other with desperate fingers. They wanted to make sure I was really there, that I had truly come back. Even Chip came down and joined our little group, like we were four people lost in the wilderness of our own sub-urban home.

I didn't tell my parents where I had been or what had happened to me until recently. They asked me, the authorities asked me, everyone asked me, but I never said a word about her until others starting coming forth. I couldn't tell them because the truth would have shattered them. I could never tell them that I had willingly walked away, left be-cause I wanted to. The misunderstanding would have been worse than any horror or abuse I had supposedly suffered.

"Why did you leave the party? Why didn't you tell someone you were going?" What would I have said to them? Could I have told them about the artificial hills and what those hills did to me? Could I tell them about the desolation, the barrenness I sensed at the heart of the neighborhood, at the chemical plant, or in the way our yard almost perfectly matched every other yard for miles around? I saw every kind of therapist and counselor you could think of, and I never told any of them the truth. I had sympathy for everyone concerned. It was my duty. But I wouldn't tell them my secret or the truth behind my leav-ing because I wasn't ready to speak it. It would have come out prema-turely, half-baked. I respected the truth too much and it really had very little to do with me. I was just a small participant in its much bigger design.

So our close family got even closer and I was viewed . . . how? With a little fear and respect, awe even. Yes, awe. They didn't quite know what to do with me. I knew my life could be different and I was waiting pa-tiently for the time when I could live it the way I wanted. My parents loved me but their love couldn't protect them from the truth behind their lives, my life, Chip's life, the lives of our neighbors and everyone else who chose to live that way and the ones who had no real choice in how they lived at all. The only difference is that I left, I walked away on my sixteenth birthday.

Mom seemed a little less intent on making everything perfect after I got back. Dad didn't stay as long at the office. Chip was caught driving across someone's lawn in our brand new suv. The upheaval of my brief disappearance had been subsumed but there were traces of it everywhere, whispering my name. And there were no birthday parties for me after that, no gala affairs. No, I would go for a brief walk on that special day, and Mom would watch me from the doorway, planted there like a shriveled tree. But I always made sure to come back, though I didn't necessarily want to.

Then a few months ago I went to a college in the east and had a string of boyfriends. None of them lasted very long. I kept a small apartment off campus. And I never went home unless I absolutely had to. I don't see my parents very often now. I don't want to go back there. I don't believe in it. I know that sounds harsh, but it's true. And now I am free. Almost. Almost free. And wherever I go I carry the promise of spring because it's inside me. And sometimes that means leaving everything behind.

Nathan Webb

If you drive by me and I do not wave it is because in one hand I hold a bronze crucifix and in the other a picture of Mary crying for her lost sheep, which is me and you and everyone who has been looking for her all of our lives. You drive by and stare at me because I am out in the cold in my orange parka when the wind is minus ten or the heat is coming off the sidewalk in waves and you see that there's something wrong with my face—like it's a jigsaw puzzle not put together right—and for this you think I am slow because of my sign that reads "The Pill Kills God's Children" out in front of the abortion clinic.

You think I am a little strange. You hesitate to come up to me. My crucifix is five feet long, with a long wooden handle that I tilt on my shoulders just so, because if it hurts God's back one time, it hurts it for all time. And what of the babies thrown into plastic buckets or wrapped in clear plastic—what happens to them? What happens to their budding souls crying out to be saved? I hear them as they are wrenched from their mothers' wombs; the wind carries their voices because it moans, and sometimes it is Christ himself crying out on the cross, "My God, My God, Why have You abandoned me?" I watch those who drive by me. I see their faces. They will not forget me, they will not forget the cross that touches the roof of the sky. My work is to stand here so they will not be forgotten, to bear up the cross that is in me. The war has only begun and you are a part of it. Someday you will have to choose sides, and there won't be anywhere to hide.

Sometimes people honk their horns and yell at me, sometimes they wave, and sometimes they curse and make obscene gestures or throw things, or yell "Terrorist! Fanatic!" But I am not a terrorist. I am only trying to do God's will. I live on the corner near Our Lady of Sorrows Church, where a dead girl was found. I live with my aunt, who is almost a hundred years old. Sometimes kids drive by playing their loud music and I can't see their faces because the windows are dark. But I see their heads; I see them bobbing in the cars, heads with hats on them turned backwards. I sit in the dark on the screened-in porch and watch them drive by on summer evenings. My neighbors are white and black and Mexican. They walk by at all hours of the day and night. I light my candle and say a decade of the rosary and watch them. I see the trash bin on the corner and pray for the unborn children who are thrown into dumpsters just like it. Sometimes in the middle of saying the rosary I stare at the trash bin and see through it to the gallons of blood and babies that had no chance to live; then I feel old, like my skin is dry and wrinkled with no chance of being smooth ever again. If you step on a crack you have stepped on an unborn child; if you see a torn black trash bag hung up in a tree you are seeing an unborn child; if you look at tiny creatures under a microscope you are looking at unborn babies. Everything I see is an unborn child.

When I'm not working at the supermarket carrying out people's groceries or ushering at church, I take up my cross and picture of Mary and walk the two and a half miles to the abortion clinic, my feet walking in the footsteps of the Lord to the place where young mothers go in and come out plucked of their divine fruit, their bodies like dark empty warehouses where precious life used to be. I see their private parts as doors that have fallen away into the darkness. Their young, pretty heads of hair are nests of hay about to catch on fire. I bleed to pity them. The walk to the abortion clinic is made up of holy seeing, the air full of God's messengers swimming above my head. I am just a seer. I go to the place where the bleeding starts and never stops, the doctors wearing bloody rubber gloves they use to get rid of the babies with, wiping their shoes on the mats that say "Welcome" before they go home at night to fall asleep in their big easy chairs. If I had the power I would let them hold the weight of this cross, have it bear down on them, and I believe someday their hearts would melt from all the killing and they would get on their hands and knees and repent and crawl back into holes in the ground. I believe they would. But inside the clinic, where I have been only once, it is cool and bright and clean and no one can smell death because they have a way of getting rid of it. They clean up the air by pumping in false oxygen.

I used to take pictures of every girl with a Polaroid camera until they made me stop. I see their fear and shame, and I give them names and ask God to please forgive them. Jackie, Beth, Cindy, and Sally; Susie, Crystal, Eve, and Mary Anne; Betty, Annette, Kim, Louise, Tara, Ally, Jessica, Judy, Rosa, Grace, Bridgette, Sara. The pictures are tacked to my wall at home and I pray for them. Some of them have pierced ears with holes that go all the way up the folds of their skin, with shiny, bright jewelry—and some of them look like they've come out of a terrible dream. Sometimes I am in their rooms where the baby is being made, sitting in the corner with my cross, and I see their naked bodies moving in the dark, and that's when I hear the babies begin to ask for God's love in a sound just below a whisper. But they won't live long enough to become a voice. They think it's themselves alone even when I am there with them, but Christ is above us all watching as the child's forehead is beginning to burn itself into the mother's stomach. I am there with them. I watch them make the baby. I love them, even before they murder a child, before he has a chance to be an apple seed and grow into a tree. I love them.

Once I was in the park when my mother was still alive, and I heard the leaves calling my name and I looked up and saw a chorus of angels sitting in a tree. They were not bright angels, but dark angels, and I asked my mother, "Can angels be sad?" and she looked at me like she saw something for the first time, and she said, "Yes, they can." And that's when I knew I was touched, and my mother knew it too, even if I did have to take special classes at school. She said I was blessed and she loved me. I saw the dark angels and they were weeping and mourning for those that will never be. I wake up in the middle of the night and a voice says *Do what you can*, and I take up my cross the next day and walk to the clinic and hold it up and pray.

And the strange weather of the clinic, the way they hate me and the way I love them, the way the unseen currents go back and forth swirling all around us, and how they want to reach out and kill me—and how I want to reach out and hold their hands and not let go—all of us making a circle that will never end. It just won't end. You can't hate what is God's, you can only hate what you have chosen not to give him of your own free will. So I wait and do my duty, which is to stand there every day as long as I can. Some days I am there for over eight hours. I walk back and forth for many hours, praying over and over again, "Lord Jesus Christ, have mercy on them," until I don't know where I am and the sky above comes down into my eyes. The cross is heavy, like heartache on my shoulders.

I remember suckling at my mother's breast when I was an infant, how the warm blue milk flowed through me like light, and I remember looking up into her eyes and seeing God, and this is why he put me on earth: because I remember what it was like being born. The light and darkness are one, not separate: I see the plant, the seed, the dirt, and everything as a whole picture, not just a part of the picture but the picture itself, with the wind behind it also a part of it and the falling and growing light and its highest point along with its lowest, and each and every part of this same river working beyond time that is not time because God does not die and was never born. That's why I get dry sometimes, for what I see as a whole and not as a partial thing as others see it.

I stand here, day after day no matter what the weather is, and the young girls keep coming; they do not stop, their pregnant bodies keep adding to the land of the unborn, until I see the babies' heads like small gourds or pumpkins piled one on top of the other, stretching out endless to the horizon like the same quality stones to pick from. They're like eggshells that wait to be crushed by your feet. I eat my Snickers Bar and think about the waste and how no one can do a thing about it but wait for the hour of His coming. I have been thrown in jail and suffered the abuse of my coworkers at the supermarket; I have been beaten and spit on and congratulated. If there was more of me to give I would gladly give it. The light keeps getting brighter and brighter, and then it grows dark as the dark angels swoop in to take over the night. I do not sway in these convictions.

I would not kill the doctors who kill the babies, only ask them to eat their dinners at night bathed in the blood of their innocent victims. I would ask them to shower in that same blood and take a bath in the afterbirth that never was, just mucous and dead baby brains of those who just wanted a chance to think on the glory of God. The dark angels say "Amen" and shudder like a windfall of crows. I will stand out here until I die. It's why God put me on the earth. I want to see where they take the murdered children so I can scoop them up into my loving arms. I want to rescue their remnants and show them to anyone who would open their eyes and see, who could bear to witness the truth of this massacre. I would take those dead babies and lash them in plastic bags to the top of the cross because they were crucified before they ever had a chance to be. Where I stand the weather is cold or very hot and the hill slopes down to the streetlights and the cars fishtail when it snows, and I feel the snow land on my face like cold feathers before they melt. The air in winter is so quiet you can sometimes hear yourself breathing. When I pause in my march and my feet are tired, I look up into the white sky and see the flakes of snow falling from the clouds, and I think just for a second that maybe, just maybe, all of those dead babies are coming back to rescue us from ourselves.

Moffut Townsend of Miami, Oklahoma

I don't care what color your skin is as long as you fear God. When I caught an Indian scratching "White Man Go Home" in one of my bathroom walls with a broken bottleneck from a Thunderbird, I skedaddled him out of there pretty good on my braces, going at him like a pair of giant knitting needles in your grandma's gnarled hands. His face was cratered like the moon, and the way he looked at me was like he was Brother Crow and I was the branch he shit on. What I would not do for a clear-eyed view of this nation's history.

I sit here and sometimes I try to scratch below my knees where my shins used to be, and this makes me feel hollow and foolish because the limbs you once had are no different than those you have right now, if you're lucky enough to have them; they still ache, they still feel like the blood is flowing through them, and if they fall asleep you still have panic for the part of you that doesn't have feeling. This is why I think of where this country is going, because I see every color under the sun pull up to my station, ask for a key to use the bathroom, which I clean myself every goddamn day, and I see that the mirrors I installed in those glorified shithouses reflect a face you would not want to meet, not here, not anywhere; and they are like the itch I know I shouldn't have but have anyway in my phantom toes, festering in the wound, and it makes me restless when I know they're in there when my feet are not, my feet out wandering around in a dream-field somewhere, cut off from the rest of my body, mocking me and the God who made even them. And this causes me no small amount of grief because I dearly want them back, attached to the rest of me. I am an honest man with a small business to run. I don't even consider myself a racist. I take you as you come, but if you come to deface my store, why then I will shoot you and not think twice about it.

Goddamn the pain. Goddamn it. Why should I continue to have pain for limbs that are not there, for feet and lower legs that are a part of the wind now, or a cow's bell? Why should the hot fever of limbs long defunct continue to cause beads of sweat to break out on my forehead? Is there any way they could be brought back to me, like the man who took up that dead girl's bones and took them out onto the open road? Why doesn't he come into my store, I would surely welcome him, as I know what it is to have parts of me cut off and gone forever? Their story gives me hope because the girl's bones are alive again, and maybe they can be for me, too, for all of us who are damaged and afflicted, lost to ourselves. My missing limbs make me sweat sometimes on my crossword puzzles, or the legal pad I'm doodling on.

I dream of them sometimes: What are they doing, leading me to a stream where I can feel my white cotton socks hug me as they touch the ground, lift up, sink again into the soles of my shoes? Sweet touch of earth, like coming home. Then I'm a complete man again, I feel solid, of a piece, no herky-jerky movement anymore toward the freezers in the back like a man-sized windup doll. I take my painkillers and sometimes I fudge: I take more than what's prescribed, but doctors don't know anything you go through on an hourly basis; they don't care how the seconds drip by between doses, how you learn to live for those doses in their milligrams of relief, because pain is not living, it is only the raw fingers of a fire licking you until your bones turn black. *Their* legs aren't missing. That's what I mean about the pain that's there for limbs that are no longer.

I whittle away at the doorstop with my pocketknife, curving designs into the heel of it, small curlycues announcing the coming of *the pain* like some ruthless god. I wait for customers to come in and ring the little silver bell above the door, which is like a small chorus of tinkled warnings: either it sounds like hope or it sounds like doom. When I have not taken my drugs it sounds like doom. I get restless and irritable and I watch the clock and see the second hands circle in slow, awful arcs like a sundial arching across the yard; I sweat it out. And sometimes, it is true, sometimes I do say, "To hell with it," and I go whole-hog and get lit up like a Christmas tree.

What anguish, this double kind of life.

What would you do for the relief? What would you do? You would sell anything you had, any bauble that's worth a dime, nostalgic or otherwise; you would do what I do and get it any way you could because only the pain is real and everything else is not. For the drugs, I mean; for the relief. It's like an empty room, the dimensions of your mind. Dust in the corners, light cutting through the blinds. I can't put it any other way. You reach a point where there is no hope and then what do you do? I try to be honest. But I'd do anything for it now, it has worn me so far down that it's the only way I have for marking my life: shoot up, hit, come down; shoot up, hit, come down. Keep the pain at bay, manage it like a ball team that keeps losing. This is what *it* does to you because *it* can, and there is nothing else, just *it, it, it*. I miss my goddamned feet.

I remember the flood in '87 when the river rose and became orange and the whole Oklahoma landscape was an orange tide, like the rivers of Mars let loose over the plains, soil churning in the water as we became buoys for waves that were always rising. Miami was an outpost in an alien world and we were all alone in the northeastern corner of the state, our community swept under as the color orange itself seeped into everything, wicker chairs and swimming dogs, leaving it all painted in the colors of the setting sun. I still had my legs then, not doing secret dealings in the backroom with a nineteen-year-old dealer with earrings that say "Star" in silver letters. You could see where the river passed by, the rake of its passage; tree trunks and parked cars and hillsides and houses had horizons burned into them where the water reached and no higher, like nature's own painting of the apocalypse. It was sundown on them, always sundown wherever the river passed and left its mark, ringed with caustic dusk like the lights of the world going down and becoming water. The river bathed everything in battery acid, and I remember how a mailbox was oranged up to the top of its post, like burnt smog or a painting of some country setting. It was postcard beautiful in a doomed sort of way.

Spoonbills floated in the tang, belly-up and bloated, like gigantic bars of sickly white soap turning in the mire clockwise and counterclockwise, the second hands and the hour hands all wrong as they spun to show how even time itself came undone. Fish cannot survive orange water anymore than they can see through the clear casings of their own eggs. And if they are no longer fish, what are they? I have not fished once since the time of the flood. Dead carp and spoonbills just kept coming, tumbling over embankments in the silver kayaks of their bodies and, "Lord, help us: this is new," each of us said and dared not repeat, and we did not know how to pray to a god that let his water turn orange even though we were responsible for it.

It was not the end of the world, just the end of what I knew or believed about rivers, which is almost the same thing. With it came my diabetes and the unraveling of my life until here I am, an honest man in my fifties, squeezing a goddamned rubber ball between cold shakes of heroin withdrawal for feet, Lord knows, that are not even there. They are not even there. It don't make any kind of sense. Me, a respectable white man with deep Christian roots who has lived in this part of northeastern Oklahoma all my fifty-eight years, a drug addict and commiserator with pond scum: it don't make any kind of sense. Not a day goes by that the force of that incongruity does not hit me stump between the eyes. If that janitor dug up the dead girl's bones, why can't he bring my feet back to me since him and she been popping up everywhere? I'd welcome him, I know exactly what I'd do: get around my counter and get down on my false knees (because they're all I have left) and I'd ask him in the name of God to please, please bring back the rest of my legs for me. Restore me to myself. If you can raise a girl from a terrible murder you can do a small errand for an addicted old-timer like me. Find and bring back those legs so I can walk straight again, a whole man once more.

Because I used to be a smart man, well-read when I had the time, reading every western novel and history book there is. But what am I supposed to do now with the knowledge I been given in the form of my addiction? I pray to the Almighty God to send me deliverance in a form I can tolerate because I am my own opium den.

"Evenin', Mrs. Meddlestone: brisk out, ain't it? Well, you can't tell nothin' about weather in Oklahoma that it won't undo if you give it time. Yes, it is a bother, sure enough, and don't you look nice in your pearly white dress. Need a hand with that? I'll jes hop on over and give you a hand. What brings you out upon a fall evening? How's Claude doin'? How's that back of his? You betcha I like petunias, you betcha. No need to worry about finding that change, it's just a pittance. Say hi to Claude now. Good night, nighty-night," and other chitchat, until the words coming out of my mouth belie my true condition, which is a cat dancing on a corrugated roof after a lightning bolt. I smell smoke, I tell you, smoke; my bowels are on fire.

Did I know then what was in store for me when I woke in the middle of the night, crazed with thirst, and the river beyond each window rose to meet its orange deliverance? Did I suspect my affliction was some-how a part of the river, and my own coming addiction beginning to heave and surge like a stream overflowing its banks inside my blood? *Townsend*, I said to myself then, *Townsend, you are thirsty because you cannot help it, and even if the thirst burns now it's going to be all right and the orange river will go away.* But it did not go away. I was the king of rivers in my waking nightmares, swallowing that contaminated wa-ter and thirsting for more. I could not drink water ever again without thinking about this orange. I was thirsty and still do not know why, though the doctors have told me all about the sugar levels in my blood and how they fluctuate; I have the clinical part of it down cold. What they don't get is that the river was *inside me* the moment it broke its banks and swallowed up the town to become the only thing I know for sure, and I am an honest man. I believe in God, so help me God, I do. The baseball field at the college was a lake of Martian tides with poles sticking out in the outfield, and this made you want to shut your eyes and start over somewhere else, anywhere else, only there's nowhere else to go because you're there. Our babies swam in this same water in summer, swinging from tire swings, and we drank and took showers in this water, and why it should have turned that color no one really knows. Maybe that's why they cut off my legs: because this part of the country needed an orange flood, though God knows what for. Personal dignity is not all that makes a man.

I give my money to the punk dealer in the back room where I have stacks of office supplies, staples and paper towels. He calls me Moff and I stand there shaking like a flag. It's not that I want to shoot up, exactly, just that it's the only thing I live for. If only he would bring me back my feet, if only he could do that. The light above me flickers in its fluorescent tube, like a moth trapped inside it is trying to get out by tapping and flapping in soft plinks against the glass. I am that moth, and I know what it feels like to want to both escape that light and submerge into it, let it consume me like a monk. He counts off the bills in front of me, and each time it's the longest five seconds in my life; they come out of his hand like furls of green smoke, and they're not as crisp as they should be, they're tired, dead lettuce, and our transaction has the seedy quality of someone coming to collect an overdue bill. It's me he's collecting, only me, and what he does with the receipt I have no idea. Please, God, save me from the brush of his kid's mustache and his swinging ponytail and his wallet chained to his back pocket and his backward ball cap and his sly grin, like I'm in his wallet too, which of course I am. I want the leafy bills to go away and leave me alone, and I close my eyes as he counts them off; we are like lovers who can't stand each other anymore but are going through the motions. I have never hated one person more in all my life.

I have an addict's mouth and an addict's wrinkled skin. I smoke Pall Malls nonstop. It couldn't be otherwise. Drunk Indians come into my store and nigger athletes from the college with their fake gold jewelry dangling around their necks in chains, hoping for the big time. We're all one country, right? Each time I tied that tube around my arm and shot up, wasn't the river coming back for me? Wasn't it the tide that's always rising? Mistake it for blood or Jupiter's wings or whatever orange conjures in your mind, but do not mistake it for a freak of nature but rather how nature is supposed to be. How nature is. I do not want to be pitied. I forbid that. I am an honest man and keep a clean store. I'm on the side of the winners, not the losers. My people come from Monroe, Alabama, and we settled this country. They're buried five generations deep into the ground. And some people say it's the last gasp of the white man, but see how we go out; see what burning is really all about. You haven't seen a riot yet. I lost my feet and they're still walking around somewhere, looking for a skull to crush. When I shoot up good, when I hit that vein and the shit for once is good, I start to levitate, and then who needs feet? Nothing touches me because I'm floating, and just for a brief precious time I hear music in my head that is not music and I am the grand floating maple leaf and my transparent skin shines with light and hey, hey, I'm lighter than a goddamned feather.

The store bell announces their comings and goings, a warning sound, a welcoming sound. Tins of starfish tune are stacked neatly and gleam in their pyramids, the one item I wish folks would not buy because of the way they look from my catbird seat. I have a shotgun under the counter—and I've stroked its walnut stock once, maybe twice, nothing to get excited about. Just grazed it with my fingertips, telling without saying, "Go on and try it." I have everything you need, and I see people come into the station, or lean against the panel of their car, and wait for it to start filling up. I look out the window. I see them staring off. I watch the cherries of their taillights fade away into the rising dust. Why not the janitor and the dead girl? Why not? A few more hours now and I can lock up the store, and then I can go home to the kitchen table. There I cook the shit up good and wait for it to take me away. I miss my legs. They're out there somewhere, in some incinerator, ash of my ash, in black dust that blew away when they opened the furnace door, that used to be bones that lived and breathed and moved. Maybe the janitor could bring my feet back to me. Maybe he could just so that in another life maybe, in another dream, I can walk upright out of my own place as a man should, with my shoulders square into the sun, my habit kicked once and for all, humming "Amazing Grace" and thanking God for making me whole once more.

Little Woodpile

Gone, because Mama said it had to be, gone 'fore it ever was, she shakes her head and I lick her stamps as they take out the burnt couch—"Careful now"—the one I set on fire, the one where Mama lay under Mr. Dean Robbins with his full weight on top of her, their soft cooing in the dark, like she was the center of the earth and he was digging to get there. "Mmmm," Mama says, "Mmmmm." Panting, sliding, cursing coming out of his throat, I smelled and saw the couch before I burned it. I am a good boy and Mama can tell you that. It is burnt black on one side while the other side still has the pattern of daisy flowers I loved to see.

Mama calls me Woodpile because of where I like to hide, in the shade of firewood out back of the toolshed. When I was little I went there to get away and hide in the early afternoon, behind sticks shaped like the steeple of a church, where they could not see me but I could see them, Mama and her men friends. And the owls hooted somewhere in the sky; I heard the blowing laundry of their wings as they flew by. There were beetles in the dirt and sometimes I ate them to see what they tasted like, and they were like glass bits around tiny sores. Mama sat on the swing on the back porch and drank lemonade, her long white skirt cool in the hot afternoon, drifting with the swing, the man taking off his hat and wiping his forehead with a handkerchief. "Sure is hot," he'd say, and Mama'd say, "Sure is." Crickets sang under the porch, and I waited for them to go inside so I could feel sad and cry, making mud at my feet.

They angle it through the door, stop, back up, put it down, rest, pick it up, and shift. One of them cusses low in his mouth. It's a long couch, like they're taking the house apart piece by piece. I wish they would take the door down and everything that leads into it. The smell of rain comes close like a hidden sheet, and Mama shakes her head and will not look at me. She will not look at me. I lick another stamp. I am thirty-one candles today; I will have a cake and Mama will light it and the candles will flicker and I will blow them all out in one big breath, like whoosh. They do not look at me. They do not look at me. I saw him straighten up suddenly and take himself out of her, jerking and shuddering. "Rise up and deliver your pillar of salt, ye Jerusalem," the preacher said. I am thirty-one candles; the preacher said I am a moan, a divine creature of God, and a death knell.

I took the poker from the fireplace, the one shaped like the top of a metal gate where the rich people live, and I came up behind him and raised it above my head so that the shadow on the wall looked like it was growing into a tree. Mama opened her mouth and he turned around and both their faces, so soon moaning sacks of the couch's pleasure, pleasure I could not name because I had no way of getting there, became screams before there was any sound: the scream that always was, that is waiting for me at the bottom of my throat. "Billy!" Mama yelled, and I dropped the poker and it clanged on the wooden floor. I did not hit him. I did not bring it down on his head. He smelled like sand at the bottom of the river, where things just go to sink and die without sound. His face hung loose on his jaw, like a door swinging in front of a dark house, and he was surprised to see me standing there, as if he suddenly saw everything that ever was, his own life and my place inside that life, about to take it away in just that moment, how pinecones fall from the trees without sound in the blood-red forest, and the highways shine with the paint of killed deer, and Mama's fancy stamps of Glenn Miller, and the wheels of circus lights turning when I was four, *pretty, pretty,* each became a part of the mask that was his face and fell away until there was nothing else.

I walked back to my room and closed the door.

They whispered in the dark, but I couldn't hear what they said.

A rustle of clothes and the back door slammed and I heard the empty bowl sound of his walk and then he stepped off the porch. He got into his car on our long gravel driveway, drove away and never came back. Then stillness, quiet, and our house rocked alone in the dark. I heard Mama sobbing, but I did not go to her. Our house became one big sobbing, and after awhile I cried too and Mama rushed in with the smell of him still on her, and she rocked me to sleep with her tears pouring out and we were safe from another distance.

I lit the couch on fire. I took the matches from the kitchen drawer, wrapped a stick from the woodpile in newspaper, and lit it on fire. It ran up the back of the couch like the torn yellow tear of a dream, eating everything. The fire rose up and touched the ceiling, curling under it like a wave. They came to see Mama, because Mama is pretty and *commands an audience,* and I heard them from my bedroom. I have a fan on the ceiling, and with each turn of it I heard them laugh softly then start to moan and the couch was a part of it, the sinking part of it where they were on top of her, breathing dragons, and I lit it on fire. It felt right. It felt fine. The fan did not stop. I said, "Burn up now," and carried the fire from the garage before it burned my hand, while Mama was outside. There's a prize inside her stomach, some prize they were trying to get, like marbles or a stuffed animal or cookies you eat on a cold winter day. Digging at it with their hands and hips shaped like a jar. I could not go there.

I saw a burning tree when I was little and it looked like how I felt inside, where not even Mama can touch, a hot place looking for small twigs; fire that builds and protects me, fire that burns me down into smoking black grass. I could not get my wooden blocks to burn, though I blackened them like the couch; I could not get them to become those angry faces I see in fires that let me know God is on his way and already here, waiting for me to find him. I saw the looks on the men's faces, like they were hungry for sweets, and I shrank back in my room like a shriveled flower with my matchbook in my pocket. I looked at my hands. "You stay in your room, Woodpile," and I did. I prayed and buried my head under the pillow, but Jesus wasn't there.

I think our house is a wooden boat and Mama and me are the oars. I think we go out to sea every day and do not catch a fish.

When I lit the couch on fire the room started to glow, and shadows jumped up like dark clothes and danced and kept on getting higher, with small bright sparks snapping out of the couch, zipping the air like fireflies, turning on their own lights, and my face grew hot and flushed from waves of heat I could not see hitting me, as I held the burning stick in my hand.

Mama says her favorite singer is Elvis and I believe her.

In the middle of the fire was a lake of blowing trees, and they were trying to touch the sky beyond our ceiling, and I knew God was trying to touch me and I could not see His face; I prayed at the edge of the fire before it burned me, and then Mama came in, and called the fire trucks. And *Burn, fire, burn,* I said to myself secretly, because there are no ears in daydreams. She took my hand and we left the house. And now they're carrying the couch out, cursing and sweating, not looking at me because they know I started the fire and I know how they know it and they are afraid of me, before it starts to rain.

I lick the stamps for Mama's bills, and they taste like some kind of sour soup, like my mouth is taking a bath in the middle of licking. I lick the stamps and the letters get moist at the corner where my spit makes them damp. These letters made of spit, these mouths that touch my hands when we open them. They have gone and left us, Mr. Applewright, Mr. Tom, Mr. Finnegan Jones, Mr. O'Reilly. Mama used to spend hours in the bathroom getting ready, changing herself into something they would love, some other person, her lips getting brighter as she put on lipstick like bright cherries, her hair getting curlier and curlier. I watched her from the doorway, and sometimes she'd pause and look at me in the mirror and smile. "Mama has to look nice for our guests."

Old-fashioned stamps, stamps with pictures of famous people, of Louis Armstrong and Elvis Presley and President Ford and old movie stars who are dead, the stamps of famous people, and my tongue licking them to another place, trying to get them to come back to life, sending them across an ocean I've never seen, in an airplane or a submarine. There are new stamps now that you don't have to lick, but Mama gets the ones you can lick so we can send her letters together. I can be her helper.

The couch is out of the house now. The crows are in the trees like the small dark marks you see in books. The couch is sitting in the long shadows of the porch before it rains, like it is saying "I am over now." From the window I see Mama rub her sweatered arms because the rain is coming and the men nod and shake their heads. They take it down the steps into the yard, the two of them, and Mama looks like she has a cold. Part of it touches the yard while the other part teeters on the stairs. Her nose is red. I lick another stamp and with the lick comes the first drops of rain, streaking the window, but Mama and the men do not move right away to get out of it; they just let it dot their clothes, and one of them takes off his hat and wipes his face and sighs, and Mama scribbles a small note and puts it into one of their hands, and then they lift the couch and put it into the truck and then they are gone. Mama stands in the rain, like she has been left behind. But she has not been left behind. She has me. I am here. I am here.

When you find the dead dog under Mrs. Millstone's porch this is what you do: you make sure the dog has all its bones, the bones are where you start. You make sure all the bones are there and you count as high as you can go; then you take the bones and put them in a sack where they are safe while Mrs. Millstone is in the hospital and the squares of light under the porch hit you in a criss-cross puzzle and the dog who is dead is delivered into your hands. Poor dog. Good dog. Be still now. And the dog obeys. And you move those bones wherever you can, carrying them like a secret that takes you into God's hands, because you have bones too, and someday someone will have to move them. You hide them in jars and cans and under the bathroom sink, behind the radiator where it is hot and clanks and rattles its small hammers; you take those bones to every place you know, and you put one of them under your pillow at night so that when you get scared, you can reach under and feel its sharp ridge, and maybe even cut yourself to prove you are alive. I know because I was there to find the dead dog. And you talk to the bones—their name is Moses—and you ask Moses to take the darkness of the night and the fear away, to protect Mama from all the men she has known and from especially herself, and even from your daddy who gave you a yellow truck once with a siren you could wind up, before he hit you in the eye and went away forever. You move the bones around and they make you wanna cry, "poor doggie, poor dog," and beneath your skin there are dog bones and they are big and white and fearless, shining like pieces of paper from the sun.

Now you have prayed with all your heart for these bones to be safe, and you look at the leaves around your house because you cannot help it, and no one can call you crazy no more, you're not crazy, you're not, because you see what is in front of you and not what they tell you to see, because they say you have to see it in order to be sane. Because the bones are like your bones or any bones at all.

You hold a bone and you rub it against your chin, and now you belong in the woodpile and someday it will be your turn to burn, and until then so many things can hurt you, like the cold that creeps through open cracks in the wooden house and makes you shiver all over. Where are the bones? Where are they? In the freezer. Under the bottom of the stairs. In a little pouch that smells of moss. In your hand at night, clutching it, clutching it down to where your desire is. In your closet or at the end of a piece of string. Then the bone is not a bone anymore but your deepest-down biggest wish you are afraid even to tell God about, because he knows about it already. In your heart. In the spaces where the light pours in. Your quiet is a prayer and the light pours out of the bone to fill you up. And that's how it works: a story at night you keep telling yourself over and over, how you and Mama will be happy one day, like in the beginning, and the men won't come around no more; of a cool pond where you can wet your toes; the story of dog bones, bird bones, of rabbits, possums, and people. But find the bones, and move them, move them. Do not let them go. Don't let them get covered with ketchup or the dust of old nickels. Do not bury them in one place. Do not ever forget them. Do not.

Mama walks up the porch stairs, hugging her sweatered arms. A bone is a prayer you say to yourself and it is a gift from God you have to hide. Because you don't want to scare anyone. And even though you want to light the whole world on fire you don't, because you have this bone to remind you of something you have forgot, to remind you of the yapping dog with ears that rose when he was alert and listening, like you are alert and listening. And Mama is a bone with skin wrapped around it and beautiful brown eyes that look like a robin's nest without eggs, and someday all you will have is her bones to wander around with in your hands. Be a good son, then. Do not hurt her feelings. Like the night while Mama lay with a man, I crept to my closed door and held the dog's leg bone to my face and scratched my face and cut myself with it and watched the blood trail down my skin, and that's what I became. The dog's bones was me, Mama, the house and the strange man who was trying to dig her up.

So every day for a year, after Mama left for school and Mrs. Millstone died, I watched Mama back out of the driveway in the station wagon and I went out to see Moses to make sure he was all right. I wrapped him in a blanket. I watched his fur disappear. I whimpered and cried. I cried for the dog he was, and I cried for what he would never be for me. I cried that Mama had to go away each day, and I cried when she came back. Just once did I take a bone from Moses and take it back to the house because he was disappearing day by day. I slept with it under my pillow until Mama said, "What's that smell? Are you hiding something from me?" "No, Mama, I ain't hiding anything." But I lied, I lied. I thought if I could take a bone from Moses's leg then I could scare these other men away; I thought I could shake it in front of their faces and be off with them, like Mama says to flies, "Be off with you." Because I watched them on the couch; I watched them with their pants down and Mama's pants down and her eyes were always closed, sometimes her bottom coming at me and the men going into her bottom, and I held the bone and gripped it hard. I moved the bones all over the yard and house; I planted them where they could watch everything, in Mama's garden, under the sink, under the porch, one tiny piece of bone I tried to eat and swallow. I moved the bones from place to place, and I know I will never stop moving them until everything that's bad in the world is dead and gone forever.

Lizzie Vicek

After Bud died I could write poems at the kitchen table and not feel like I was trying to get away with something behind his back, like when he was alive and I stole down into the basement whenever I had a moment to spare. I could write in the open then because he was gone.

He died in a freak accident on the switch crew with Union Pacific when he got stuck on the tracks and his body was torn in half. There was no open casket at the funeral, though the undertaker said he could put him back together almost as good as new. But I said, "No, no, I don't want to see him like that." My man was gone anyway. No use pretending he wasn't. I didn't need to see him dressed up, with makeup on his lined and weathered face, which would have been an insult to his memory. He was a man and that's all you need to know about him. I loved him more than anyone, but he wouldn't have understood my poems or why I had to write them in the first place. But maybe I didn't give him enough credit in that department. Probably didn't. He wasn't the kind to mock other people's interests, no matter what they were, but that small, precious part of me that kept things private just grew of its own accord until I passed some invisible boundary where I had to write out the clandestine poem in the basement next to the work bench and the laundry, line by line, struggling to find the words to say something I never could in everyday speech, just this secret burning thing I had to do, though neither one of us finished high school or ever left South Omaha. Who knows where these things come from anyway.

I live in the same gritty neighborhood we first moved into almost forty years ago, though now it has Latin and Korean gangs vying for supremacy, the gradual shutdown of the stockyards after generations of my family kept coming over to work in them from the old country, from Bohemia. Now it's all these meat-packing plants and a wasteland of empty warehouses. Every other day one of those gang kids comes striding up the street like he's greased for trouble, some beautiful Mexican half-boy half-man, with his pencil-fine mustache and paisley blue bandana wrapped around his head, doomed for jail or worse, walking like a cat or a subtle haze of slow-moving smoke ready to disappear into the atmosphere or blow up, as some other kid down the street sits in his low rider waiting to shoot him. That's how it is around here and getting a little worse every year, especially in the heat of summer, the houses close to each other with no yards to speak of on the crooked streets. Sometimes I hear three, four gunshots on a single night. But kids around here don't pay too much attention to an old lady like me, so I just stay out of the line of fire.

Move? Where would I go? I had the kids here and Bud remade the house with his own two hands, room by room, board by board. Our life was made and broken in this house. I've known no other since I ran away with him. I don't care that my poems have started to show up in high profile magazines and that I'm getting some attention. I'm not going anywhere because that would be like turning my back on everything I ever was, everything I come from. So I live and write here, minus the kids who are grown up and gone, and Bud who's been dead for decades now.

When I first started to write poems the kids were still in school, and between them and my job at the Schlitz factory, which is shut down now, and taking care of Bud, I had almost no time or energy to myself. Never enough of either, too little of both. I believe the phrase is stretched to the limit. Throw in haggard, too, and you get the picture, so many other women like me—and men, too—you could shake a stick at us. Not that I'm complaining, only describing how it was. So I wrote when I could, on scraps of paper and grocery lists, or waiting in the check-out line at the store with Jeannie hanging off of me, a line here, a phrase or image there, just enough to keep the fire burning. "Why write at all if it becomes that hard and desperate?" someone asked me once, and I couldn't answer the question except to say, because I had to. As Milosz says, "Endurance only comes from enduring." I had to, and that was all there was to it. Sometimes after making love Bud would set up on his elbow and say something searing and true that made me want to blurt out all kinds of things (though I didn't, I was hard on myself that way), "Lizzie, there's a part of you I won't ever be able to reach and this makes me sad and also makes me love you all the more. Don't even try to deny it."

So I didn't. He was a good, decent man that way, far-reaching in his heart. And of course he was right, dead on. He knew something was changing in me even then and he wanted to go there with me, but he also backed off and didn't press the issue because he knew I was all for him and he was all for me, except for this tiny part that had its own private life that had to unfold in its own way. Bud had his own dreams that had nothing to do with me, and they never had a chance to come true. He was a helluva left-handed pitcher with a nasty fastball at South High, and I fell in love with him in the tenth grade and that's all she wrote. Two kids by the time I was nineteen, just a few months out of high school, with three more on the way in rapid succession. 'Course Bud wanted to pitch in the major leagues, but he blew out his arm at the end of his senior year and that was that. He couldn't get that fastball back no matter how hard he tried. This was back in the day when you couldn't rehab the way they do now; he just come up hurt at the wrong time in sports medicine. He never did get over that, the death of his dream—and when the College World Series came to town we went and caught a couple of games at Rosenblatt every year, and that was when he drank the most, to remember and to forget and to think about what might have been. The last thing I wanted to do was to tell him about poetry—not after raising the kids and making a life together. There was no precedent for it in my family, or in his, for that matter. So I kept it to myself.

So I was born a second time at thirty-two after coming across an Edna Saint Vincent Millay poem on a postcard tacked up in a Goodwill store, of all places, when I was out looking for cheap summer clothes for the kids. It stopped me in my tracks, like I had known those fourteen lines my whole life but never had a chance to realize it. You know how that is, harried beyond belief by kids that need and need you like there's no end to it, and you're just slogging around on errands because no one else will help you, and, frankly, no one cares. I don't know why this little piece of writing on blue paper caught my eye, but I could hardly drag myself away from it and kept coming back with tears of gratitude starting in my eyes. But thankful? Thankful for what? For seeing a poem taped up on a store window surrounded by other fliers and announcements, some tiny scrap of insignificance? But it wasn't insignificant to me, and that's how it was and how it happened, getting born a second time in broad daylight and at the Goodwill, no less, myself a mother five times over by then. I was pretty much a goner after that and found myself looking for tiny cracks and openings in the course of a day, five minutes here, ten there, a whole half hour sometimes, just to get something down.

"What you doin' in that basement all the time, Lizzie?" Bud asked me once. I didn't have the heart (or the energy?) to tell him the truth, so I lied; I lied and I'd like to think that was the only true lie I ever told him (but I know I'm fooling myself on that one). But it was the biggest lie, the most conscious one. A poem about the dragon's tail tattoo on his right forearm, how it made his skin some tragic burning message of the promise of his life—the one about Millie, and the scar above her right eye which she got when she went out to look at the stars, to collect what pity there was left in the cold, cold universe. The poems were about them, but they came out of me—and when they left and wrote themselves on the page, there was nothing left for me to write about but move on to the next one and the one after that and the one after that, about the way light rises and falls on the gourd high up on the shelf. And so it goes on for a writer, any real writer you can think of, this burning obsession to get something down you can't even quite call your own, though sometimes you dearly want to claim it and other times you want to say you had nothing to do with it at all.

Then it happened one weekend. I had the whole house for a day and a half because Bud's taking the kids camping, and I told him that this one time I was too tired to go, so just go without me. He was disappointed and so were the kids, but they left on a Friday afternoon, which meant I had that night and the whole next day to myself. I waved to them from the porch as they pulled out of the driveway, waved in open and not-so-subtle betrayal, because the truth was I wasn't tired—or rather, I was no more tired than any other time, but I said that's what it was, the reason I didn't go camping with them. You have to understand what an empty house meant to me then, like a furious, lovable army pulling out of occupied territory. I felt guilty for exactly two minutes, went back into the house and just sat there, my heart both calm and excited at the same time. What would I do all by myself? How would I pass this empty day and a half? Are you kidding? I would work on poems and try not to think about the family I loved so much coming back, and how the prospect of them coming home nearly made me want to run away. Once or twice I would start to open my mouth on the subject of writing, just start to make shapes around the words I knew I couldn't say, and those words just up and died on me, which was a merciful thing. The last thing I wanted to do in the world was hurt them—or worse, confuse them—with things I couldn't talk about, coherently anyway.

Mama wants to work on her poems now; Mama has to write poems because it's seething in her blood, because they're just as real or more real than you are. No. I promised myself it would never, ever come to that, and I kept my promise. But that weekend, that weekend. I stole into it like a ship coming into harbor at night under a full moon. Now when I go to writers' events and things like that and people want to ask what writing poems means to me, I think of Bud and my kids and just politely change the subject. No use going into that because there's no way to describe it, even if I do write poems. I'm not above being rude and just shutting down that line of inquiry altogether, because I can't expose them that way.

So I made myself some coffee and smoked a cigarette or two at the table, humming inside myself like some floating golden bar, and set to work on the legal pad I had stowed away in a special place. And I just wrote and wrote and wrote. Wrote clear through the night and into the next day, pushing myself harder than I ever have before or since, writing against the clock because I was counting the minutes and the hours before the family I both loved and dreaded came home. Pushed the pad aside only after I reached that tired, cleaned-out feeling to light another cigarette. And another one. And another one.

And that's when I saw them, Jesse Breedlove and a neighbor girl named Twyla Harp, who later died in a car accident.

Out back of the house is a small alley with a gravel road and an upturned oil drum next to a shed. Jesse lived down the street and his dad was a drunk, his mother even worse. He must have been fourteen years old or so back then, and he knew and sometimes played with Carl and Steve before they went their separate ways. I haven't thought of Jesse till he got into the news for making off with that dead girl's body—haven't thought of that troubled kid for decades, though he was always in the back of my mind, lurking there in the shadows. He'd be about thirty-five now, same age as Steve, maybe a little older. He always was a strange and serious kid, like something was gnawing at him, like he was cut out for a difficult life (though it's easy to say that, after everything that's happened). Here I am, spent and wasted after a burst of writing alone in the house for the first time and about to go up to bed, when he and Twyla Harp show up in the alley carrying this odd bag of trix that would later come to haunt me. Now the thought of them and this bout of writing have become one in my mind, fused at the core of their deliverance, two kids who believe it or not played at putting birds back together, which I'd come to know about so well, dead little birds with bright colors pressed into the ground or lying where death had dropped them, their eyes poked out, sparrows, hummingbirds, and finches; birds that could fit into the palm of your hand like balled-up muscles of flight ready to burst forth. They tried putting their bodies back together again (can you picture two children so in love with the world they even wanted dead animals to come back and join them?) with popsicle sticks, pins, and junkyard wire until the birds stood up like laughable, avenging angels on skinny, improbable legs.

The little stage formed a half-circle of pathetic and threadbare birds atop the oil drum, their open beaks so severe you could almost travel down the source of a silent scream, some of them with rosary beads for eyes. (I saw him plant one, with delicate care, like dropping a seed into the earth, into the dried-out eye socket of a robin.) And what tenacious grip on life was this exactly, what harbinger of things to come in a working-class neighborhood in South Omaha? The stockyards even then were starting to close, so the stench of livestock was not as bad. I saw something bright and silvery shaking behind the trees when those kids had passed, and I went to have a look because I needed some fresh air. Somebody's streamers, a used car salesman's vagrant tinsel, caught in a thicket? But no, it was neither, and I went to investigate because, well, I don't know exactly, except that its brightness drew me out, got me going in a certain direction. Pulled my sweater tight around me, rubbed my arms.

The dead birds were smeared in swaths of red, blue, and yellow paint, like the garish flag to a forgotten country, bands of color like caged bars of the afterlife. It took my breath away: they stared at you with open beaks in a half-circle, six dead birds got up in a kind of war paint with wings outstretched, some of them patched together with needle and thread, waiting for you to cough or otherwise break the spell so they could devour you. I didn't know whether to laugh or cry or be outraged. For some reason they didn't even smell. It was the strangest tropical sight I had ever seen, and it blinded me. Threaded into their breastbones were glittering fishing lures whose barbs were studded with candle wax, lighted when they brought matches.

I was more astonished than if I had stumbled upon a primitive tribe in the middle of the city, a tepee or a smoke hole. Cellophane for windows, porches on cinder blocks. It stopped me in my tracks. They were dead birds, just dead birds, but arranged in such a way that there was no way of turning back without being changed somehow for what you had seen. I tasted the colors when I saw them, and I wanted to become the birds, grabbing my throat with a sob and wondering how on earth these children decided to communicate with the dead in just this way. I mean that troubled boy Jesse, the one with the long black hair who was bounced around from home to home in South O and later haunted the Southside bars, shipped off to God knows where and coming back more taciturn and tattooed than ever, higher-strung than a violin chord. You could see the tendons in his neck tensing when he was walking down the street, staring straight ahead into nothing. He could have been my son so easily, maybe in a way he already was. And the girl, sweet little girl, Twyla Harp, with long auburn hair and blue eyes, who died in a car wreck on her sixteenth birthday. Maybe he never got over it and it catapulted him into his strange and wandering life, so that he had to dig up that dead girl in the cellar of a church. I don't know, some people are cut out to be alone for the rapture they felt once, for the way it burned them up.

I went back inside, shut the door, and sat down at the table in a daze. Lit another cigarette, of course. And that's when it happened, when I knew in my bones that I had to write poetry no matter what. It was Jesse Breedlove, who was so dedicated to putting those birds back together, like he was rehearsing for resurrection. He restored wings to birds that would never fly again, and I just couldn't understand it (though I did, I did). He led Twyla down the gravel path behind my house in the muddy rutted alley, and she followed him in her yellow sundress speckled with mud and her oversized jacket lined with imitation fur; quite a pair, those two, off to see and remake their birds. I started writing poems about them at my desk whenever I could, following their forays into the birches where they remade birds and lit up the world, if only for their own eyes and mine. After that first afternoon I was their secret and vigilant witness, watching them look both ways before they stole into the trees, Jesse leading her and nervous even then, their locked hands like a brief stab of mercy. It was mercy they were after, and redemption, and they were searching for it in the only form they knew (dead hidden dead birds), and if you can't recognize this then you are barely alive.

Once on my day off I followed them at a safe distance, and watched them crouch beneath the oil drum, shivering and naked as they smeared mud on each other's chest in gestures so slow and genuine it was like they were remaking each other's body in the clay of a soil that didn't have a name. To touch someone like that . . . to mean it . . . Whatever happened to that boy later on must be mitigated by this, that the power expanding inside of him then was simply too much for him to bear. A weathercaster? A lawyer? A man who worked for the city filling in potholes? Are we talking rapture or the sorrow coming out of the workaday world? Because whatever you think of him, if you think he killed that girl and buried her body only to resurrect it for his ghoulish practices, think how much he loved this other girl, the one I knew and saw, and those other delicate bird bones that do not have a place in your heart unless they are arranged to strike terror, awe, and reverence into it. That's who we are at the breaking point, when we have to face the moment we've evaded all our lives.

I wrote about them in a draft of a poem called "The Bird Makers."

> The first bird directs its fire
> into your mouth
> and with its gaze decides that you, the watcher,
> must go; The second bird is water
> and drowns you in its waves, which rise and curl up
> like a young girl's hair when she has closed her eyes
>
> Now you are the birds you see,
> and fly up with the knowledge of the emptiness
> inside you, wide open seeing
> going on forever.

That's why I followed an orange striped tom one day into those same birches and shot him with Bud's .22. That's why I walked out again holding the dead cat by the tail, because who knew I would care so much to the point of killing something else? I surprised the cat just as he was about to jump on the drum, and the moment is frozen before me: "Git!" I yelled, and it did not git, just raised up on its back with its fur standing up, and I knew then that I simply had to shoot it. I took dead aim into its hissing mouth and shot it dead. Maybe that's why I write poems: to celebrate this rundown neighborhood and people like him, the reason you are reading this right now, because he's wanted for abduction and murder. I write them because Bud's been dead a long time now. I write them because I live alone and walk around and see that a Latino gang has spray-painted my mailbox. I have no goddamn idea why I write poems. More importantly, it's the boy and the girl, their love for a world that has already vanished; of resurrected birds stalking me like something out of Stravinsky's *Rite of Spring*. And if you had a choice whether to avert your gaze or surrender to the birds, what would you do? What would you do?

On the last day I ever talked to him, I followed Jesse into the birches; he stood alone, open-palmed.

Why do you do it, son?

The birds stood on the drum like creatures from a prehistoric age, and I pictured them parting long wet grass with tentative beaks. He took out a fifty-cent piece and started bouncing it on the top of the drum—where he could have gotten it I have no idea—and it made a sound like something hollow resounding in the middle of my chest, and the birds hopped a little to the vibration of the large silver coin and his insistent beat, hopped a little higher each time, turned themselves to profile at different angles so I could see in their eyes and they could look into mine, like you'd see in Indian rain dances sometimes, long-laced moccasins licking the air and the beat of the sheathed foot poised on the edge of an invisible circle in the middle of a chant you could not name.

Are you running from something?

And the coin bounced in its bright, silvery percussion, and the birds jumped a little higher until I thought I almost heard a cry coming from their mouths, and maybe he wasn't holding a silver coin after all but the droplet of a star, a disc that grew brighter and made the birds dance and leap about, until I saw their wings start to work in their death joints and the birds on top of the drum grew gracefully into themselves and tried out their wings, though they didn't fly away.

Can you tell me what it means?

I threw everything out of the house I did not need after Bud died, going through all of his stuff and giving half of it to the Salvation Army: flannel shirts, flasks, tools, knives, knick-knacks of all descriptions, spoons and forks, pillows, sheets, light fixtures, hub caps, the extra coffee maker, mounted fish, work boots, his chained wallet, wood carvings. I was crazy for two days, determined to get rid of all of it, to peal away the layers of my domesticity and coordinate a new kind of life, simplified, more austere, where maybe I could, after all, start writing poems in my own house where my husband and me lived for forty years and then he died.

Bud, did you think I was composing grocery lists down there after I worked my shift at the foundry? I was trying to write poems, poems you would never see because I loved you too much and could not bear to be found out; it would have been worse than having an affair. Dear God, what we can never know about another person because we're afraid to share it, and they wouldn't know what to do with it if we did. I mean the aloneness, the rapture, the isolation. I know how your hands planed this house, worked the lathe, went into the porch until the porch became just the extension of your hands, and when I sit on this porch I sit in the open palm of your hand, and when you lost your right pinky because Jeb called for you and it was cut off in the saw. Maybe it was your finger on the top of that bird, asking me to come closer ("Why didn't you ever show me your poems?"), but I don't have an answer for you, Bud.

There's a part of each of us we just can't share, and I'm sorry about that, I'm really sorry about that, but that's the way it is. "Why didn't you ever show me your poems?" is the question you must never ask, even in death, because I don't know the answer and you do not even know why you ask it. This is where love must begin and all certainty end; why those dead birds, dancing to the beat of a silver coin, trumped my own love, because Bud wouldn't answer me even if I could ask it all over again.

I started to say something, and stopped. The boy left. I never went back to that charged place, but I thought about it all the time. It's still in my dreams, like a Chagall painting trying to rearrange itself. I know true awe when I see it, and that boy knew. I don't think he killed her. I just think he wants her to live again for a reason no one can ever say.

Pompadour Williams

They dragged the river for my body and did not find me. What they found was a man who only looked like me, except he had a toupee clinging to his skull and my hair is real, rumors to the contrary. They found him some ways down the Missouri, that shit-kicker brown river, down from the casinos in Council Bluffs, and pulled him out in his cheap seersucker suit, which probably became a net of underwater stars, and I suppose there was mud and grass in his mouth, I don't really know. But I have dreams about the man who wasn't me, who was supposed to be me: I see his bloated body and grotesque face and he is trying to say something and he spits wet vegetation out of his mouth; he is trying to tell me what it's like to lie underwater, weighted down with sandbags, staring up at the surface, and the terrible beating that took place there. They didn't even know why whoever it was killed him. I see his face sometimes when I turn around suddenly, in a crowded supermarket or department store. Is he calling after me? Did he finally find me after all this time? It's the dead man, Harold Banks, my Doppelgänger, coming for the man I wasn't and the man he was.

I was drinking gin in a cheap motel room halfway across the country in Reno when they suddenly flashed my picture up on the screen, dragging the river for yours truly; rarely have I laughed so hard or so bitterly to the point of tears. How in the hell did I make it on TV? They thought that other son of a bitch had killed me, done me in, and no doubt they were holding him as the primary suspect in a murder case, *my* murder case, only he didn't kill me. They found out soon enough. In the meantime they put my face in the papers in black and white, said I was missing, but I wasn't there either, even down to the toothpick I had in the corner of my mouth since I quit smoking; even my dyed red hair, which is really white, but you do what you can. Nevertheless. I'm here to tell you I'm very much alive, breathing right here, my pinky ring glittering with five diamond studs. Seldom is a man given a chance to disappear; I was given that chance and I took it. There are tens of thousands of missing people in this country and for a time I was one of them, though in actuality the only thing I was missing from was an affair gone bad. I took up with my thirty-year-old secretary and her husband found out and got on my ass. He was out to kill me, leaving death threats on my answering machine and fucking up my car, and I finally just thought, *I'm too old for this shit*, and I disappeared.

I was selling hearing aids at the time, had a nice little office in Council Bluffs overlooking the hills, an expense account, silk shirts, but I was bored to tears. Bored, bored, bored. It's always the same thing: I move to a different city where nobody knows me and try to start over fresh, only to end up with a woman who gets me into trouble. Or, rather, I get myself into trouble—there's no one to blame but myself. Some men like to hunt, others like to gamble, still others play the stock market, but the only thing I ever got excited about was getting a woman to fall in love with me. Then, sooner or later, I'm out of there, like air sucked out of a vacuum. I suppose you could say that's my real calling, pathetic as it sounds, getting women to fall for me and then leaving them when the bloom is off. I'm not proud of it, but there it is. It's not like I keep count—I sure as hell don't look like Robert Redford—but I'd have to say I've done this fifty times or so, maybe more. It really isn't a conscious effort on my part, just a gradual sea pull in a certain direction until off we go to late dinners, holding hands, sharing hushed confidences, whether she's married or not. You could say it's in my nature. I'm not proud of it but we're all made for something, and I'm made for having drawn-out love affairs.

I work hard to get them to care about me, and sometimes even then it doesn't pan out. But it isn't for lack of trying. First I notice how they hold their hands and what they do with them, how they hold up their chin, for example, or cradle a wine glass, or stroke the edge of the table, because sooner or later (though I don't think it at the time) those same hands will be touching me. And whether they have polished nails or not, delicate fingers like silverware or a nurse's hands, it's the motion I know is coming that soothes me and at the same time sends a thrill up my spine. So the hands are the starting point, and no two pair are ever alike.

Her father, the previous man, her ex-husband, her current one, is the object of your sorrowful disdain and shaking head, because it's painfully obvious he doesn't understand her and she deserves so much more, and even though you're not quite in a position to give it to her, you're moving in that direction, quietly, reverently, and she can sense that. You both can. This isn't an act, can't be an act because you always have this idea in the back of your head that maybe this is *the one* after all, the one you're going to settle down with or run off to Vegas in a rented convertible with. If all you're thinking about is getting her in bed to get your rocks off, you're finished before you even get started, before the physical part is even on the horizon. For me it never is.

So this is how I mark my life, by how many women have said they love me and meant it. How do I know they meant it? I suppose in the end it doesn't really matter; even if it's just for that moment they mean it, and that's all I can hope for. Maybe it makes me feel real and not the two-bit shyster I really am. I don't know. I simply become the sieve of her worries and desires and fretfulness, holding her up gently in the dignity she deserves and treating her like an angel; there's no one like her and never will be again. It's like a tune played only once, in a certain key and chord change. Of course nothing that beautiful can ever be sustained because people always want more, they always want to keep on hoarding a good thing until they squeeze it to death without knowing it, and then it's gone. I just recognize the signs sooner than most.

I've been told my pursuit of women is pathological, that I have a sickness. I've been told a lot of things, by husbands and boyfriends and other women. But who is fooling who if you can't admit that love dies, or changes so much in shape and form that you can't even recognize it anymore? It's too sad for most people to handle, to admit that they're really alone, that there is no such a thing as a soul mate but only soulful times, smoking in bed together (when I smoked), "Let me get that for you, sweetie pie," or watching the rain race down in streaks on the window, holding each other close in the early morning hours.

I love women: I love the way they smell and I love the way they move, even some of the not-so-pretty-ones, and the sound of their nylon panties rubbing when they walk or cross their legs. A slit of a woman's dress, that brief flash of flesh when they walk by on the sidewalk, is a glimpse of heaven that brings me to tears. I love their hair and smell and nipples, which feel like erasers in my mouth when I gently tug on them between my teeth, and I love to see the cleft of their chins raised in ecstasy when I go down on them, like the prow of a beautiful ship. Their bodies are temples, and you better go there to pay some serious homage. They don't have to have hour-glass figures, and some of the best in bed are those who don't even look it, just as those who look it are most often all facade with no real passion underneath, dry as dust. None of this is planned, it just works out that way.

Is there anything more fleeting and petal-like than a glance from a curious woman to show you she's at least aware of your presence? I'm no saint but I'm no hypocrite either, and if she looks at you, even glances your way, you're a fool not to act on it. Other men have sensed what I'm about and hate me for it. But it's themselves they really hate, because they don't have the gumption to acknowledge a woman's interest, which is sacrilegious to me. Or, rather, they're threatened by me. Not just jealous husbands either: any guy who senses what I'm about, doctors, lawyers, truckers. It's fear that renders them mute and paralyzed, and I don't give in to that fear. I have no problem making a fool out of myself if I at least sense I have an outside chance, and even sometimes when I don't, when I know I have a snowball's chance in hell; let the chips fall where they may. What did one comedian say? A man is only as faithful as his opportunities?

So I took up with her, my last great fling before I put myself out to pasture, and that led me to the story I have to tell you. Her name was Susie and she was beautiful, a real knockout, with huge smoldering brown eyes that were tough to read, like she was either keeping her temper in check or getting ready to fly into your arms. The kind of Latina-looking gal that beats a good-looking blond cold, with a certain hue of skin somewhere between exotic desert country and an explorer's pith helmet. She was about five-foot-nine with long, dark hair ribboned down the middle of her back and nice breasts the size of apples. And her legs . . . Jesus, what can I say about them? A bend in the river, high dunes, another world where her calves were smoke made flesh and led up to the tight hills of her beautiful ass, which barely quivered when she walked. Even for a jaded old buzzard like me she was pretty spectacular. We had been working together for maybe four months when I called her in one morning. "Susie, could you come in here for a second?" and I swear to God I really did need her for something, a missing check or some such thing.

She came in in her open-toed pumps and black tailored dress, with red-painted nails just so, and I said to her, "Do you know where Mrs. O'Connor's refund check is?" And that was it: she looked at me in a certain offhanded way, and I was hooked. I knew she was only twenty-nine and married, and I had sworn—as I had sworn so many times before—to just behave myself and grow up, but I couldn't help it. Something was starting to rev up inside of me already. She wasn't even remotely interested in me at the time, I was just a guy she worked for, and she said as much three months later when we were staring up at the ceiling after we had just made love and I was huffing and puffing like the old fart I am. "I don't know what it is about you," she said. "You're old enough to be my grandfather." Then I turned her over and proceeded to lick every inch of her body with soft, feathery strokes— for two whole hours—until we both whimpered and cried and I had to get a massage the next day just to get the kinks out of my neck. She tasted like the inside peel of an orange dipped in rye, only it was less strong and much more elusive; it was orange-like, faint and reminiscent of blossoms in Florida.

That was the beginning of the end because there was no way it could be sustained—it would have killed me anyway—and somehow her husband Darrell found out. I suspect she broke down and told him, because she really was a good girl, had only ever been with that dipshit, though God knows why; they'd been high school sweethearts or something like that, and he looked like a hillbilly just out of his shack or a second-rate stock car driver with grease under his nails. I came along at the right time and treated her like nobody ever had or probably ever would again. She was a wildcat in bed, but that's not why I loved her. I loved her because she didn't even know what she was capable of, how passionate and smart she could be, how much was out there just waiting for her to discover. I knew how to love her and take care of her and I say it without pride: if there is another man out there who can treat a woman like I can, who will make her the entire focus of his universe every waking moment, then I would gladly shake his hand and move over. But I haven't met him yet, and I don't think I'm likely to.

Anyway, Darrell blew out the back window of my Lincoln with his shotgun one rainy night in March (who the hell else could it have been?) as I was reading about John Huston in my easy chair, one of the few nights Susie and I weren't together. We were pretty much together constantly at that point. I closed my eyes and knew. I suddenly felt tired and old, like a dead spider that curls up into a ball and just blows away. I looked at my hands, my sun-spotted, carefully manicured hands, and that was it. I retired—and never again would I would chase skirt like I had, like I was possessed by an inner demon that commanded me to *Go after her, Go after her, Go after her,* even if she throws a drink in your face. My life's work, such as it was, was done.

And what a helluva relief it was. To finally reach the end of the line, to know I had given up and that that trail was behind me: all I had now were memories and, you know, they can sustain you sometimes, if you're in the proper frame of mind. Darrell, that hillbilly bastard, had set me free. My only real fear now was that he would hurt Susie, and that I would be responsible for anything that happened to her. I couldn't take that. I made up my mind to get him out of her life, even if I wouldn't take his place. I remember Susie telling me stories about Darrell, how he yelled at her sometimes for not putting a coaster under a glass or for throwing her coat on the couch (turns out, ironically enough, he was a neat freak), and I thought to myself, *Can't two people ever really be happy together without that kind of petty shit?* The answer is no, they can't. I sighed and proceeded to make love with her for the rest of the afternoon, until I thought my heart was going to burst. The only response to nonsense like Darrell's is to make tender, crooning love and let the memory of that trash wash away.

I didn't stage my own death, it just worked out that way. I knew Darrell was out to fuck me up and God only knows what he would do to Susie. I went to their neighborhood the next morning and sat in my car at the end of the block. Some neighbors were out in their yards, milling about. It was Saturday. I saw him come out the front door, and in plain view of at least four people I drove up slowly, got out, and said loud enough for everyone to hear, "I have been having an affair with your wife, and if you touch one hair on her head I'm going to have you put away." Darrell went berserk. First he punched me in the mouth and sent my dentures flying. Then he called Susie a whore, and she came running out into the yard in her bathrobe to get between him and me, and he kicked her in the groin and she crumpled to the ground. By this time I looked up in a daze to see that he was ready to brain me with, of all things, his own mailbox, which he had wrenched from its post. Luckily, some neighbors intervened and wrestled him to the ground. "Darrell! It's not worth it!" one of them said. There were a lot of people around now, and Darrell was crying and cursing, and Susie was rocking gently back and forth in the yard.

I later learned she had a miscarriage—and maybe it was my kid and maybe it was the Neanderthal's. But I'll never forget the sight of my kitten on the ground moaning in her silk kimono bathrobe, with tiny white socks that looked like cotton swabs on her slender, beautiful feet. Even as they were leading Darrell away he was screaming things at me, spitting in the air, and one of the things he clearly repeated again and again was how he was going to kill me. Well, oddly enough, I felt a kind of relief. After they took him away, I crawled over on my hands and knees—and what a sight I must have been, a turtle without all his gums—and made it to my little baby. "Susie, sweetheart, beautiful . . ." but she didn't say a word. So I held her, I just held her, and I don't know how many watched as we became our own little life raft rocking in an endless sea, where it felt like every eye in the world was watching us and wishing us the worst kind of harm.

Did I feel bad for breaking up yet another marriage? Did I have some remorse? No, I did not. Not even close. Not in this case. She deserved more, she deserved better, and I was just the agent of change, you see. I guess I taught her that. I took her to the hospital and that was that, my last great romance ending as they so often did, in numb silence in an emergency room. They put her in a wheelchair, but before they led her away I took her face in my hands and raised it to mine: "You're gonna be all right, Susie, better than you've ever been before. Get out of Council Bluffs. Start over somewhere new." I kissed her on the forehead and in that moment, even after all the passion we'd shared, she was my granddaughter, and I would never think of her sexually ever again. Because I'm not a pig. I am not a pig.

They fixed my mouth as best they could, and then I left. I left everything behind me, even my Lincoln, because for some goddamned reason it didn't start up again when I stopped at a convenience store. So I just walked away from it; it's still there, for all I know. I got on a city bus with five hundred dollars cash in my pocket, transferred to a Greyhound, and bought a one-way ticket going west. It's so easy for me to leave everything behind. I've been doing it for forty years, it's like one of the seasons. I wish people would understand that. Like stepping off a stair. I left a half-full glass of water on the nightstand beside my bed, a closet full of shirts and shoes, ticket stubs from the dog track on the kitchen table, a rubber hound dog I got from God knows where. I just left all of it, rode off into the sunset with just the clothes on my back, intending to drink myself to death. And you know what? The only thing I think about to this day is that half-full glass of water on the nightstand, how long it must have stood there before someone came and emptied it.

Did it grow algae or did it remain clear and still to the end? Did it collect dust or insects or a fleck from one of my own eyelashes descending from somewhere? Was it waiting for me to return, to drink the other half—or would it always be a clear, still pond that hinted at a better world? So that's what I really left behind: a glass of water and the memories of Susie, who deserved so much more that I feel it like an ache sometimes, that someone so young and so beautiful should be so unaware of what life has to offer because she was tied up with an idiot who drank beer seven nights a week and was addicted to pornography. It just didn't make sense. And what of those other women I had been with—Betty, Dre, Sarah, Kelly, Joan, Mary Sue, Linda, Lisa, Annette . . . Jenny, Dianna, Sasha, Erin, Taylor, Margaret, so many beautiful names and faces I could not keep track of, until the memory of each of their faces formed just one woman who was the beginning of a new world where I was pilgrim, explorer, and correspondent? Were they hopeful in life or bitterly disappointed? So much depended on the answer, *my life depended on the answer*, and I cringed to know which way the chips fell. Because I was largely responsible for the outcome, any outcome, and you need to know that; you have to know I made a difference in a helluva lot of women's lives, and they won't forget me. I know that now, and it makes me shiver and it makes me quake. Those moments are my one true offspring, my only sons and daughters. I was made for being alone, ultimately, which is exactly what gave those precious weeks and months their power and vividness: I would end up alone and I would die alone, which is the only time, the only time, when I wished I could have stayed with just one.

So when I saw myself on the screen and I saw Darrell's mug shot next to mine, I had to laugh because, finally, I thought, here's a quirky bit of justice, just a bit, to suggest that sometimes fairness does win out after all, and here's the proof. My guardian angel, who has had just about the worst assignment God could ever give someone, must have laughed, too, wherever she was. I say I gave up chasing women but that's not entirely true. I stayed inside that motel room for ten days, long enough for the police and the FBI to drag every pond and river around Council Bluffs, and in that time I drank like a fish and didn't venture out much. *Whatever happened to that goddamned glass of water?* In fact, I got real sick. It was the end of the line for me. I knew what failure was and I knew what it tasted like—like old, stale ice cubes. I was prepared to die, you see, to just fade quietly from the very thing that had been plaguing me my whole life: a broken heart.

As I got sicker and sicker and continued to drink myself to death, I imagined having conversations with this river-grown underwater man, this phantom who followed me wherever I went: "Tell me about your last night on earth, Harold, and who you managed to piss off. Tell me your story and I'll tell you mine." But he didn't say anything back. I watched the looming shadows of people pass by at all hours of the day and night, people drunk and laughing, people fooling around on their spouses in cheap motel rooms, as I sat alone in the dark with the sound on the TV turned off and watched them pass by. Did they think they were getting away with something? Did they think this was the last word? And what a pathetic pageant it was, the worst kind of laughter and desperation, because they would have to wake up tomorrow or in a few hours to a stark new day, and they would already be a little older, filling up with a nameless regret that wouldn't catch up with them tomorrow or the day after that. But someday it would find them and hunt them down, even if it took twenty years. I noticed how their shadows got larger the more they moved by my window—which was maybe eight feet long—like they were moving into the curves of these shadows, growing into claws, becoming the night itself and part of my alcoholic dreams. Where was Harold, where was my personal dead double to comfort me or to taunt me?

Then one night toward the end of it, a long-haired fella checked in to the room next to mine. There was something different about him, but I didn't know what it was. He was carrying a heap of something wrapped in blankets, just another transient on his way to God knows where or nowhere at all. I spied him through the plastic curtain as I revolved around my drunken and invisible stem. Whatever it was he had hauled up looked precious to him, that's for sure, because he handled it with care and kept looking around. Later I heard him murmuring through the walls in a way that cut through my alcoholic haze as some kind of urgent and necessary speech. He was talking to somebody, but I had no way of knowing who it was. Didn't sound like he was on the phone. I paused in my drink just long enough to get interested. I kept thinking of Harold then, and how he had died, a small-time, two-bit gambler who owed another small fry some money: what a pathetic way to go, getting dragged out of that ugly brown river by the nape of his jacket, hauled back to dry land after a swim with bottom-feeding carp. I bet his shoes looked like clown shoes, I bet his eyes bulged in his head. He wouldn't answer me.

Whoever was next door to me was on some special errand, I felt it more than I knew it, and I was just reckless enough to want to know what it was because I had nothing in the goddamned world to lose. I stuck my head out of the door and saw a bright burning light seeping out of his room, a light like I had never seen before. Only later did I find out who he was, after I saw a picture of him tacked up outside a store somewhere, the man who'd dug up that little girl and took her on the road. Then I passed out before I took another step and somehow burned myself something fierce—to this day I have no idea how—and then it was the smell of my own singed flesh that woke me as I sat rocking on the floor back and forth like a lunatic egg with eyes. This is how I ended up, this was the story of my life. No more Chorey Le Beaunne, no more tulips and black-clad waiters and silk sheets where she waited for me with open arms. Now it was incontinence and death in a place where nobody knew me. A fitting end to a vain life of failure.

But I had fun, didn't I? Sure, there was no denying it. And know what? I wasn't afraid; or, rather, the fear inside me gave way to something else, something beginning to glow with a vague but persistent light. It wasn't the light I'd seen coming out of that wanted man's room and it wasn't the light inside my own: it wasn't even a light I could name or describe. But it brought with it a low humming sound barely above, say, the brush of a feather on a hard wood surface. Just a brush, a stroke, a delicate lapping sound, like maybe seaweed at the bottom of the ocean moving to the rhythmic pulls of the current. And suddenly I realized it was my own tongue inside my mouth that was making the sound, the same persistent sound and motion so familiar to me in the act of cunnilingus, but it wasn't working on any woman's private parts now, only licking carefully, dutifully the bare skull of Harold Banks without his toupee, licking the top of his head. He was sobbing and we were both underwater, and his skull tasted like marble with a touch of salt. Out of the vague, murky water a thousand eyes started to watch me clean his head with my tongue, and soon enough I began to see it was every woman I had ever licked, who gained their mermaid bodies watching me with careful devotion, as a hand would come out gently once in a while to move my tongue a few centimeters over on Harold's skull, because for some reason I didn't have hands and was just the extension of my tongue unfurling across the plates of his marble skull. All these women were watching my performance, and Harold continued sobbing. I licked his skull for hours on end, I was all tongue, and I felt a ripeness in my chest even in the dream, as if my heart were a piece of hanging fruit ready to fall off the tree. It had all come down to this, to this one act of charity underwater, where a dead man and my ex-lovers came together to show me what I really was: I was cleaning another man's skull with my tongue, lapping away at those hard plates that contain all our dreams, hopes, and fears.

Harold's skull was getting brighter now, a green-tinted hue, and he continued to murmur and cry. So I was not really a lover of women after all; I had been evading my true calling all of my life. My real vocation, my real calling, was using my world-famous tongue to scrape away another man's pain, to get at the marrow of a haunting, and give a murdered man some peace, the man who could have, should have been me.

I'm sorry, Harold, I did not recognize you for who and what you are; I'm sorry I laughed when they found out it was you and not I who was killed and thrown into the river. I didn't know the real reasons for the terrible mix-up, why you had to die and I could go on living. Your skull was the cleanest surface I've ever tasted, and I hope it did you some good, even if it was just a dream. I tried to love as many women as I could, but they all got away from me; to love just one properly would have been enough. I think it was Judy who told me it hurt her pelvis to make love. We did other things instead, and I was gentle around her rickety frame. They found me face down in the motel room, and revived my heart with CPR. I live where it's warm now, but just yesterday I got a postcard from Susie with two sentences: "Dear Gene, I got out of Council Bluffs like you said, and I'm no longer with Darrell. Thank you for all our times together—I won't forget you. Love, Susie." So something good came of your death, Harold: I gave up chasing women and one of them, one of the best, started her life over after a difficult time. I don't know why I ended up licking your skull, maybe it has something to do with forgiveness—the man who killed you, the women I hurt, Darrell's mistreatment of Susie, the guy who checked into the room next to mine, probably with that girl's body. My wandering and woebegone life. Looking back, it all makes sense now, why you had to be killed and thrown into the river, why I fell apart, why the love I always sought could not be found at a woman's feet, or through anything else whose main imperative was always running, running, running, from this lonely heart to the next.

Earl Dodson

I drive by mesquite tangled like a sea of barbed wire and Joshua trees staring at me in their ghoulish poses with my window down doing 80 mph, and feel the sunburn creep up my arm. Starting to peal already; too fair-skinned for this climate. Scraps of glittering debris, aluminum cans, and shards of broken glass shine from the side of the highway, and yet eighty feet from the highway only geckos skitter across the sand to keep me company, or tiny bright red birds that suck on desert flowers. Then, just for a second, I feel like I'm way out in the middle of space, completely out of the loop.

I'm chasing a phantom, a figment of my own and the public's imagination, which flickers in the half-light of some gathering dread. I and all the law enforcement agencies of the country trying to piece together a motive in a good old-fashioned manhunt for a janitor turned fugitive who dug up the body of a murdered girl.

Who is Jesse Breedlove? Why hasn't he been found?

The road is beginning to wear on me, and I miss Janey and the kids.

Too much Mexican food and "Ultra vez, por favor," and fleabag motel rooms with bad air. I've been at it for five weeks now with no real leads as I talk into this recorder and the miles fly by, little cantinas and painted cacti on the sides of liquor stores like bad cartoons, with sombreros and banana hands and devilish mustaches curved like whiplashes. Mitch expects a story in three weeks, but all I have are supernatural accounts of encounters, quasi-cannibalism, people turning into crows, and hallucinations; apparently, Breedlove has a wax candelabra in his chest and the dead girl sings a slow blues with her mouth sewn shut.

There's a story inside every story, like there's a story inside this one, a kernel inside a kernel, and I will peel away the layers until I find you, Jesse. I have no choice now. You're in my blood. *Who are you? Why did you run? Did you rape and kill her like they say?* This might be as close as I ever get to you, driving across the hot wastes of nowhere, talking into this damned thing (which is like talking on a one-way line). The grooves of the highway moan like a steady dirge or hum that leads nowhere. America is like that sometimes, and I'm tired. Janey doesn't understand the need for a story like this; she thinks I chase ambulances, which is pretty close to the truth. "Why do you want to turn him into a celebrity?" And what's the point of saying it wasn't always like this, that *I* wasn't always like this?

There was a time when I wanted to write—really write—and get down to the nethermost of things and people, Lorca's dark root of the scream, where you touch on the universal truth of things because there is no other place to go or to be, and words become the only things keeping you from the abyss even as they take you closer to it. I still believe in the power of words, even if I'm not able to write them. One little compromise led to another little compromise, and compromises went on higgledy-piggledy to propagate and lead me here to the mournful truth, which is that I sold out, I cashed in. I couldn't try to be that kind of writer anymore, it was too much.

So how in the hell am I ever going to get this story down if I can't talk to you, Jesse?

They're saying all kinds of things about you: that your black eyes are deep pits of space, threatening to break out; that once somebody looks into them, it's over. But I need proof of these sightings, hard evidence. I can't write a story about a holy ghost. You're a string of fantastic anecdotes, wish-fulfillments, folk tales, cliff-hangers, UFOS, sexual innuendos, tabloid excuses, and outright lies. Some say you're the conscience behind the American psyche, whatever the hell that is. You're the story I'm after, the story of a lifetime, how to get back to America's first principals, the ones that went AWOL.

But maybe you're just another poor son of a bitch who didn't make it and couldn't take it anymore, one of the voiceless millions, some sorry sack of shit who went berserk one summer night and took it out on an innocent kid because of the powerlessness of your own life. Weeping and moaning, Jesse. Gnashing your teeth. I've seen it before. You spent six months in the brig for stealing plastic jewelry from a Thai whore, and when the Marines kicked you out you drank yourself out of a marriage and six straight jobs—all of them menial, all of them because one day you showed up (or didn't show up) cold stone drunk, murderous, and mumbling to yourself. "He was like a fucking zombie," one of them said at that landscaping outfit. "He picked up a spade and tried to hack off his own foot." You've been in the tank so many times they don't even bother to book you anymore. Then you dig up the girl after two years like a cur looking for his bone, and now you're being parlayed into some kind of anti-hero who's making people's hair turn white. *Who are you, Jesse?*

You are not me or my wife or my kids or anything we vaguely resemble. Let the other poor fools collect you.

Some nights I feel Janey breathing in the dark more than I can hear it, and it's not a peaceful breathing, but short and ragged and care-worn; her breathing brings me closer to her than anything else in the world, even the kids. I listen for its creaking ebb and flow, its garbled and secret messages, its incomprehensible oaths, sighing murmurs or sudden yelps and squeals, and I think that if I could learn how to translate those bits of dream language into something the rest of us could use, something, anything—what it means to breathe in and out all night long in a human tide while whole villages of misfits and freaks are born and die in her head—then I could call myself a writer and give vent to her troubled dreams. But I can't get inside Janey's head. I'm on the other side, looking in. I wouldn't know how to put it anyway. Her dreams have no beginning, middle, or end. They just drop out from under her when she wakes, like a river she's been lifted from, but they keep going, waiting for her beneath every conscious thought and gesture, ready to claim her the next night or the next, ad infinitum. I've never told her that's when I love her most, when she's far off in her own dream boat and I'm wide awake on the other shore, like a moon coming up over the snowy fields. Janey. You would never understand why this is the linchpin that makes us one, when you're unconscious and I'm wide awake and somewhere, in some other place, someone has dropped a stone into a black pond and it doesn't make a sound and there are no ripples hardly, just a pucker and the stone disappears into the black water, and it's just you and me and the kids sleeping in the midst of a vague but real danger, which keeps revolving around us: that's when I have to hit the road again, when the knowledge comes looking for me in the middle of the night in our own bed, with you. I look at your temple and the stray wisps of black hair at the edge of your skull, and it's the only curve that makes any kind of sense, the only geography I want to travel. Then it's time to hit the road and I'm almost grateful, when I see into what lay right beside me in my own house, not what I want things to be, a secret knowledge building that will someday break my heart.

My training as a journalist has prepared me to look at bald facts, but I'm just another poor sucker who wants a consoling myth. I can do that, no matter what the subject matter: "Mother of Four Dies in Plane Crash"; "Presidential Candidate Speaks of New Direction." And now it's you, Jesse: "Murder Suspect on the Loose." That's what we are to these people, Jesse: a story that never stops repeating itself, a closed loop. There's an old man in a diner somewhere reading the morning paper, *our morning paper*, the one we make together, about you and your exploits and how they're after you now and cannot find you. The hunter and the hunted, that old story, that old chase. But what does it mean? You and I are just a part of the reconfiguring of their terror into something they can handle, something they can digest with their toast.

We amuse them and keep a greater revelation at bay. Maybe I should have stayed in sports, where we all knew the score, because then at least there's a clear winner and loser. I don't know anymore. So I tell Janey to put Vick's Vapor Rub on Josh's chest because he has a bad cough, but she knows that already, and she already knows what I'm going to say, which is like this news story, the one you and I are trapped in. We both know how it will end, how it has to end. Which just tells me . . . which just indicates. . . what does it tell me? . . . Christ, we have a long ways to go toward getting rid of this nameless fear.

I could be you, Jesse, so many of us could. I could light out across the country, pursued by demons, running at truckers naked with a butcher knife in my hands, screaming like a buckass banshee while my pickup truck wobbles and the dead girl in the back starts to sing—it all falls into place. You're who we would be if we didn't have anyone or anything else to buffer us from true reality, from ourselves and the sorrow we keep eating like goddamned grass. You've just had more than your fair share of loneliness. Set apart from other people, your only response is rage and restlessness. I tell Janey to kiss Josh for me at night and tell me what he looks like because he's at that tender age when such beauty will not last, it's fading so quickly, literally every day. You'll never know what that is like. Even if we can't ever have a real human conversation, you need to know that about me, if I am to write a story about you. I don't want him to end up like us, but of course he will, if he lives that long. How I want to kiss his temple or forehead myself, not just imagine it; how that kind of soft boyish skin will never come this way again, the wisps of Josh's sandy brown hair, that kid smell which every day is turning into something harder and more distant. I've been out on the road too long, too many times. Janey's right, I *do* chase ambulances. Give the people what they want. I work to support her and the kids now.

Now my words are little red wagons, Styrofoam knee guards for soccer games; they're braces and measles shots and a new awning for Janey's craft room, plastic oars, training wheels, Band-aids, action figures. You can line them up on the window sill and count them off like the kids' toy cars. They're clipped coupons and plastic dragons

and silver napkin holders like an Amazon's earrings, dead with weight
and percentage points from my total sum, each word weighing like a
bean on a drugstore counter scale. They're not long or eloquent or
beautiful but a perpetual traffic jam that keeps creeping forward. I'm a
constipated writer. My words no longer are, if they ever were, ethereal
little fairies I summon to feel smug about my talent, but tiny and blind
earthworms moving the earth one precious square inch of soil or shit
at a time. This is what I do at fifty, aspirations left behind long ago to
deal with the facts of existence. Which are: I'm a fact finder and nearly
bald, with strands of gray hair teetering out around my own temples,
and sometimes I feel a catch in my heart for no reason and I fart when
I shouldn't and I don't care. I just don't. I follow leads and hack my
way through words and eyewitness accounts with a dull machete. I'm
completely submerged in the realm of the domestic, my kids' broken
toys and my wife's penchant for leaving me stickie notes everywhere,
"Don't forget to pick up Josh from Dr. Samson's at five." Maybe I don't
want to pick up Josh at five, but I do it anyway. Maybe I'd rather go
to Hooligan's and get drunk on martinis and flirt with every young
woman who comes in and come up with dream sentences: "Jesse
Breedlove is the American soul struggling to reconcile the violence of
its birth with the fading promise of its future; that's why he carries the
body of a murdered girl." That might get their attention.

But would it matter? What difference does it make? I'm an
entertainer, like everyone else. Prose has become a treadmill for me,
and even if I did have something important to say, something people
needed to hear, who would listen?

I still have moments, though. This morning, for instance, stepping
out of the car at dawn with a chill in the air and nothing but the
booming silence of the desert and the sun like a shining aureole
around the foothills as my boots made that gritty, grinding noise they
do when I step out of a car and, just for a second, just for a flash, I felt
light and carefree chasing you, Jesse, I felt almost thrilled. The air was
so clean and clear, I could see for miles. *I wanted to chase you, all I've
ever wanted to do is chase you.* Then it was not about deadlines or word
counts but movement for movement's sake, because you're on the run

and so am I and so is everyone else, and isn't that what America is all
about, trying to outrun something gaining on us? Even if you did kill
her—and I don't think you did—and did the twisted things they say
you did, like trying to fuck her eyeballs while she moaned for mercy,
you still dug up the evidence and made off with it when it would have
made more sense to let it be. *To let it be*, Jesse. Why couldn't you just
let her lie in peace? Maybe because you didn't do it. Maybe because
it wasn't the right time. You wouldn't let her rest in a makeshift dug
grave, and this suggests several possibilities.

1. You know who killed the girl and set out to find him.
2. You're a henchman for the real killer, set off on a ghoulish errand.
3. You discovered the body in one of your drunken rages, panicked and skipped town.
4. You killed her and dug her up after two years of rotting in the ground because you couldn't handle it anymore.
5. She is a magnetic field and you're the North Pole.
6. I have no idea.
7. Have no idea.
8. Religious mysticism.
9. Eenee-meenee-miney-mo with God.
10. You're a necrophiliac.
11. You're a dark angel of reckoning.
12. You don't know what illusion is.
13. The unthinkable: you are who they say you are.

But I don't believe 10 and 12, not yet, anyway, because all I have to
go on is your mug shot and a string of fantastic accounts. Mitch didn't
believe me when I called him; he thought I was making it up. If you
are *12*, if I believed that even for one second, even for an instant, then
what in the hell could I write about you anyway? What angle could I
take? Would you put the words in my mouth, would you tell me what
to write? "He came down out of Nebraska with a raven's feather in his
hair and he told me his story, which is no less the story of us all: the
girl was his burden in this world, the one source of his moaning and

hope. He gave me a locket of her hair, and it burned in my hand like a smoking ember."

America, is this what you have become for me after all these years
of covering accidents, rescues, sex scandals, coaches
slipping cash to athletes?

I see you at the wheel, Jesse, and I see her shriveled body covered up like a lump of lamb meat in the back, and I see the smeared, cracked seams of the windshield and rusted wheel wells and the dirt under your nails and the empty gun rack, which could be the rack of her tiny rib-cage magnified out of all proportion to her actual body or what's left of it, jiggling under the tarp like beads of water, and how her skin is falling away from her bones in grisly feathers and how you check the rear-view mirror to see if she is gaining on you and,—Is she gaining on you, Jesse? Is she gaining on all of us? I know you love her, or *think* you love her, that this whole warped cataract of events is also a love story, the oldest one in the book, even if it is a shocking and grisly love.

It's the Civil War all over again, North vs. South, black vs. white, man vs. woman, child vs. grownup, light vs. dark, country vs. city, night vs. day, east vs. west, Christian vs. Muslim, the haves vs. the have-nots, people with money and power vs. those who don't have squat but their TVs. It's the same old fucking story, told from the viewpoint of an alcoholic janitor and a dead girl.

You love her, don't you? That night in the church cellar, with no one around and your empty bottle of Cuervo Gold, digging like a man possessed, *digging to get the hell out*, you dug because you had to, didn't you? You dug because you were led there by a voice that didn't stop whimpering, like Janey's voice in the middle of the night, those voices that just keep whispering all night long, "Save me, Save me?" Isn't that right, Jesse? Isn't that your defense? *You loved her.* Loved what you yourself had lost, that frail connection to another world shot through with bolts of glory, of hope shining out beyond all comprehension: epiphanies everywhere in the river of her shining hair, which keeps growing and growing, and such pure beauty that you were like that worm at the bottom of your bottle, struggling to swim up out of the depths into a new light that would kill you anyway. Maybe the old rabbis are right: there *is* grace and beauty trapped in every evil action. I don't even think you're crazy; I think you're sane, Jesse, and I think you're seeking people out who might understand you or benefit from you somehow. What the dead girl has to do with it I have no idea— more conjecture. You may have done those horrible things to her, but that's because you loved her.

You loved her, didn't you, you son of a bitch? Loved what every young girl that age has, whatever you call it, whatever you believe. You would say you love her even now. And you'll travel all over this country to find a proper place to bury her, won't you? Someplace peaceful and quiet where the wind moans in the cypress trees and there's no lack of water or flowers or hummingbirds whirring their purple bruise of wings. If not in the life you both should have had, then in the death that is hers and the one waiting for you and every one of us at the end of all this foolishness. You make my heart race, Jesse, even if I am exhausted. Remorse and sorrow are hunting you down; they plan on fucking you up with their Louisville sluggers of pain. I know it because I've heard them tapping on my windowsill, too. I want to be there when you blow, when the memory of Caroline catches up with you or you hear full register of her voice. She's hounding you, isn't she? You can't let her go and you can't get rid of her, and this paradox is making you run and disappear in what's left of the wide-open west.

If I am to get your story down, if this really is the one true story none of us can evade, then you're going to have to tell me in your best pidgin English; there's no other way. Then we'll see what kind of angel you are. Touched or not. Maybe she won't leave you in peace and this means that wherever you go and whoever you choose to encounter and blow away must somehow also deal with *their* own past; you want to scare the shit out of people, shake them up, sure, but you also want to bring them toward a common center whose fixed point is like the Big Bang or the middle of a cyclone.

I talk to people after some strange or horrific event, and if they don't see it on TV they'll maybe read my account while they're sitting on the toilet or in the diner, and what real difference does it make? Other people need you because they're lonely. We just have to make shit up or we die; we have to turn people and events into myths in order to look at ourselves in the mirror and feel some semblance of hope. And the more desperate you are, the more willing you are to take whatever weird or bizarre scenario that comes your way and parlay it into the Second Coming, or even the First, any coming at all better than Thoreau's quiet desperation, better than any talk show or home shopping network. They all want what they think you got: some kind of soul, some kind of unchampioned cause that rarely sees the light of day because people are scared and tired, scared because of 9–11 and because they don't know who *to be*, and tired because they're first and foremost people with money to buy and spend. So naturally you fill a niche, like a marketer's dream. They need you more than we do. I feel sorry for you, Jesse. We're both men who were meant for something else, something nobler: I to write words more penetrating and lasting than these for a daily rag becoming more tabloid all the time, and you, maybe, just maybe you want to live your life in the service of some other role, maybe a good soldier after all, maybe just an honest man. But an honest man does not make prison his second home, and he does not drink rotgut until they find him in a stone-coma, face down under a stairwell. If you are what they say—if you are carrying the dead around *for some reason* no one can immediately recognize—I will get to the bottom of it and tell your story.

Which is what?

Not that you are a hard-luck story, though you are that, my friend, not that at every turn in your anonymous life you haven't made the wrong choices and found yourself completely alone, with nothing more to show after your thirty-five years on earth than a borrowed navy cot, a gym bag, and a pickup truck; not those things only. Or that your mother loved and wept when you left home when you were seventeen because she raised you by herself, father disappeared, or that you came back and discovered her dead with her head stuck in the gas oven and a note that said "It's not what it looks like"—none of that, Jesse. That stuff is easy. Too easy. It's like the brief outline of your life is a setup; you're trying to uncreate yourself in the humility of lived events, a deliberate maneuver to usurp any accurate notions of you.

Why won't you show yourself to me, you son of a bitch?

Why not me, Jesse, so can I let everyone know what it's like?

You're running the risk of becoming a caricature, a form fixed in parody forever; don't let them do that to you. I'll write a book about you, I'll write about how there's still a BB lodged blue-black in your left shin, how you let the rain drip off your long black hair and the appeasement of your god, Tequila. I'll immortalize you, you'll become the book I was always meant to write, the one where the forgeries of our humanity become the timeless tragedies of our race.

I'm talking to you, Jesse.

You have your strange criss-cross scars and tattoos, and you carry the dead girl like some freakish county fair act, wavering in a noontime mirage over the desert floor. But you are not the visionary some people claim you are, appearing here and there all over the country to catapult some folks into a new awareness. You are not divine, Jesse, though no one can find your pickup, trembling from exhaust pipe to hood. You are not offering a food anyone can eat, your black eyes do not contain the mystery of redemption, and you will not save anyone from heart attacks, wheezing, or greed. Sometimes I don't want to live here anymore than you do, do not want to sell out (though I already have), do not want to be judged by what I look like or that I keep working on obscure assignments or watch TV or kowtow to the status quo or shop at Target; I don't want any of these things either. So what people think makes you special is just the disappointment of their own lives. This is a fuel greater than any crude oil, and I'm sorry for the way your life has turned out, but that is your cross to bear. You're going to have to do better than that. For it's a fact that most people in this world live on less than one dollar a day, that we are lazy and apathetic, and that at the end of the day we really don't care about anyone else as long as we have our creature comforts. Yes, these are true.

Who do you think you are?

I know the girl's hair is still growing, a corpse's hair does for some time, but that doesn't give you license to carry her around; it's not the tidal sweep of all life on this planet, or a trail of comets several hundred miles long; it's not that section of violins in Barber's *Adagio for Strings*, or a shimmering school of plankton before it's harvested by sperm whales. What is beautiful long hair anyway? Hope for the beholder, nothing more. It's outlived its own utility, a note that will not die out, and if you can't see that then you are the last true Romantic alive.

Katie LeBrun

I decided when I moved out the last time that there was no turning back. He used to hold me down and pound my head against the floor until I blacked out and forgot the world. Those were rough times, but, since you asked, I will tell you about it, if you really want to know. The love I had for him was wrapped around both of us until neither one of us could move, and *That's all right*, I told myself at the time, *That's okay*, because he's all I had going for me then. I waited for him to get home each day after watching Oprah and tried to keep the house clean because if I didn't then it would happen. Socks in the drawer, coupons inside the desk, coasters stacked like neat little plates: everything had to be in its place, it just had to be. If there was so much as a drop of spilled Pepsi on the counter he might get upset. Then I could at least sit down for a bit before I got up every ten minutes to check the curtain to see if he was on his way (he liked me to keep the curtains closed during the day). The entire house waited then for him to get home, and sometimes I thought the clock on the kitchen wall was watching me and clicking its tongue in disapproval or warning, I'm not sure which, the whole thing just made me nervous after awhile. I'd hear his pickup pull into the drive, my heart would jump, and I was a little scared and turned on at the same time. Who knows what kind of mood he'd be in?

Sometimes we made love when he got home and sometimes he'd start drinking right away, but there was always an edge to it, and I liked that—or thought I did. Because I'm only four-foot-eleven and ninety pounds, he used to pick me up like a rag doll and carry me off to bed if he was in a crazy mood, and I pretended to kick and scream the whole way, and I thought I liked that, too, because I know he liked it. I thought it was important to let him know he was in control so he wouldn't get upset or nervous. He was a good man when he wasn't drinking or having a bad day. Sometimes he'd hold my face after we were done and just kinda move it back and forth real gentle-like between his hands, like I was a kitten he was playing with, and I knew he saw stars in my eyes because I saw stars in his. We were together eight years, until he broke my arm. What did I know? I was nineteen and in love. I thought that's the way it was supposed to be; I thought he loved me unconditionally, that we would eventually move out of that clapboard rental house because he promised me and I believed him.

I even quit beauty school for him.

I liked his hard, rough hands and the way he took control. I thought that was how a man was supposed to be; I thought he was the answer to all my prayers. But one night he came after me with an extension cord he had ripped out of the wall, and I knew he wanted to beat me up bad, so I did the only thing I could, which was barricade myself in the bathroom with the telephone and call 911. I rocked back and forth on the toilet, begging him to calm down. He pounded on the door with a chair or whatever it was, and he even broke through the wall. But he's a big man and couldn't fit through the hole he made, so I was okay for the moment. Somehow just seeing his arm without the rest of his body made me scareder than anything; he kept grasping his hand for me through the wall like a monster in a horror movie. To top it all off, I was pregnant with his child, only he claimed it wasn't his, which was pure crazy, 'cause he's the only one I slept with to that point. I don't know what was worse, him trying to kill me or him calling me a whore when I was just a kid and in love with only him.

What gets into some men to make them so crazy? Why do they hate women? Why do they hate *me*? I know, you get what you settle for. I've heard that all before. But when you're not given much options you can't know the difference. So the police came and cuffed him—took about four men to hold him down—and I was taken to a women's shelter, where I stayed two months before I had Nathan. This is the life I have been given and I'm trying to make the best of it. We live in a different town now, far away from Omaha, and Nathan has my last name.

It's been three years since that night and each night of my "anniversary," as I like to call it, the anniversary of my freedom from him, I bake myself a little cupcake and light a candle and usually end up crying on the porch by myself, while Nathan sleeps in his peanut-shaped crib. I cry and think about what he almost did to me, and what he *did* do to me, cigarette burns and so forth, all in the name of love. Sometimes I don't cry and just eat my plain cupcake, at least take a bite, anyway, and remind myself how far I've come, which can't be measured in time or miles but only in what I've learned to recognize about fear, which can disguise itself as love until it has you in its grip and your life is no longer your own. Learning this is not as easy as you think, and I know it sounds strange to have an anniversary so you can try to forget what you have to remember, but there it is and it doesn't have to make sense, not now, anyway, but then again nothing ever really does make sense, not to me anymore. Not his strong hands on me, which I miss because for all their roughness they knew how to touch me, and not Nathan's black curly hair, which he did not get from me or, God knows, from him. It's harder than quitting smoking because I stopped smoking but still I try to figure out why, why, why did he do that, and why did I let him, to the point that you could just about go crazy asking the most simple questions.

There's only this life to be lived right now, and watching Nathan grow. There's only what I put in the tip jar and long hot nights on the porch sipping Southern Comfort. There's only my pathetic cupcake that doesn't even taste good, and maybe that's the point, not to make it taste good because what it stands for can't be good either. I eat to remember what I'm trying to forget. I eat because I did really love him, and love him still, though I keep that to myself. I also hate him for what he did to me. It's not how he beat me and raped me and sometimes kept me penned up like a dog, no, it's the stuffed Winnie the Pooh he won for me at the fair with an air rifle and how once when we were first dating it was muddy and he laid his own jacket over a mud puddle so I wouldn't get my white sandals dirty. And his shoulders, too, like burnt hills or granite boulders that would make any woman hot, believe me. I used to think one day those shoulders would carry me all the way to heaven, as corny as that sounds. I was in love with him, do you hear me, in love, and I know you know what it means but you don't know what it meant to me then, or what it means to me now; you can't just exchange that for something else, no matter how hard you try. The cupcake's usually not that good because I don't bake good anyway and he could have told you that himself, another strike against me.

When he beat me I used to pretend I was this little yellow flower out in the middle of a field in a bad storm, but the rain and wind did not touch me—this little flower. And you can't really beat a little yellow flower anymore than you could fly on the back of a butterfly, and that's the way I made myself get through it, to see myself as a flower some ways off, and his actions, which hurt me very much, were also then far away and this is what the counselor called "detachment." It's a word I knew and lived and understood better than any school-definition; it's a word I could taste on the bottom of my tongue, and when she said it, I thought to myself that I already knew what she meant more than what she was trying to tell me. That's how it goes with people who try to help you, social workers and such, they're outside knocking gently on your window and you wonder to yourself, *Why the hell do they want to get themselves messed up with this?* But I didn't let them in, though I learned to play the game.

His boot size was 12½ and he said they fit like socks.

I've learned a lot about myself and what not to do again, but I still hesitate to go out on the porch late at night—even the fireflies seem like a kind of warning, knocking against the lights like gloved fingers. He could be at the end of our dirt road, for all I know, or tiptoeing through the woods with a long knife, ready to cut my throat. Then what would happen to Nathan and where would I be then? Just a picture in a newspaper. He might disguise himself as a night bird or a trace of fog and drift in through the window and snatch me and Nathan up by our arms. One thing I know for sure—promise you will not laugh at me—is that he can take whatever shape he wants and become it to get to me and Nathan, that's how it works and that's what you have to know about fear, which is that it controls me even though he's out of my life, because what he did to me won't ever go away, so he's still inside me like a thorn. Sometimes it's a sweet thorn but more often it hurts and is trying to tear me up from the inside. That's how it is at the bottom of the world, when someone beats on you for a hobby.

Sometimes his blows felt like kisses, sometimes they felt like a rain of heavy stones.

If only someone would've shot him when he was young, before he got started, none of this would've happened (just kidding). I know his father used to beat his mother, and even my dad used to shove mom around: it seemed normal somehow, and it's only when you're on the other side of things that you can see them for what they are. Like I said, I didn't know the difference. I'm trying to save up money so we can move someplace else, but the tips at the Cracker Barrel aren't the greatest.

I can't tell you his name.

When the rug is taken out from underneath you, not just the rug but the entire floor and the sandals you were walking in, just plain sucked off so that you're floating in space or in your own blacked-out nightmares, it takes some time to get readjusted. I've been on exactly four dates in two years, and on one of them my hands shook so bad the guy said, "Are you havin' a seizure?" and I didn't know what he meant. I went to the restroom in this really nice restaurant and threw up instead. I remember praying over the toilet bowl. There's those jokes about praying to the porcelain god—ha, ha, ha—but that's not what I was doing. I did not pray for Nathan and I did not pray that I didn't barf on my new dress. The only thing I prayed for was for my hands to stop shaking, which I swear were in front of me but which shook as if they belonged to someone else—that, and I prayed that wherever he was, he felt the heaviness of a thousand smashed plates in his stomach, for what he did to me. What kind of prayer is that? you ask, and I can only say that it's the only prayer I knew how to pray at that moment.

One of the men I dated for awhile was older and real sweet and kind, so we were together a lot before he had to go away. He wasn't very attractive, downright comical. He wore long black socks like an accountant and wouldn't take them off during sex. He even wore a green visor you could see through on hot sunny days so that his eyes looked like a snake's or fish's eyes, combing through the water, not to eat you or anything but just to check you out. He used to take Nathan and me to see the minor leaguers play in the middle of the week during lazy afternoons, and we'd eat hotdogs and sit in the stands and time seemed to stretch forever, and it was the happiest I'd been since I was a little girl playing in Miss Maypole's backyard. I didn't worry about nothin', except who could pick up my shift at the Cracker Barrel. I don't even like baseball because half the time I don't know what's going on and don't really care, but it was pure bliss, just sitting there with him as he put his hand on my hot tan knee, and I knew, I just knew he was getting hard under those funny old man plaid shorts of his; I'd even bought a pink halter for him and a black miniskirt, just to give him a kick.

He said he loved me even more than baseball, and while I didn't believe him I was flattered anyway. He always carried around this little black leather book he wrote in and people would come up to him and ask him about scores. Charlie was a gambler and a bookie—and apparently not very good at either. But people liked him a whole lot and he always introduced me as if I was the most important person in the world to him, and for a time I was. He was never short of cash and he wasn't cheap. But, Lord, that green see-through visor: it gave his eyes a shifty look, like he was looking at you without you noticing, and I even said to him, "Charlie, why do you wear that thing?" and he just smiled and said, "Gives me a chance to survey the whole field with the privacy of my own eyes." I knew what he meant then, though I didn't push it.

Once, out of the sheer craziness of it and because he had been so good to me, I asked him to take me under the bleachers after making up some kind of weird excuse about wanting to see what was down there, and I led him by the hand to a spot where no one could see us. I knelt down and unzipped his pants and gave him a blow-job and let him cum in my mouth. I wanted to do that for him because he was so nice to me. I thought he was going to die of a heart attack as he leaned way back and his visor fell off. Just then—and I'm not kidding—someone hit a home run and the crowd went crazy. I asked him, "Do you want me to do it again, this time with mustard or mayonnaise?" and he knelt down with me, shuddering, and said, "No, sweetheart, I don't think my heart could take it." Then we just held each other there under the stands. I gave him pleasure and made him happy and that's all that mattered, not the shucked peanut shells that made tiny imprints in my knees or the sounds of people yelling and hooting and stomping their feet up above.

I guess you could say I'm not a saint, that while I still have this body that men seem to want, if someone is sweet to me, real sweet and tender, I don't mind giving it to him if the occasion is right. I don't mind making them happy. Every time Charlie and me made love I wanted to laugh when he got inside me and had to bury my head in his hairy shoulder, which felt like the inside of a big musty bird's wing. But laughter in love is good, real good: I never laughed like that before and he didn't mind at all. He was on his own erotic motorbike and he worshipped me and I let him, and it was good while it lasted. He asked me to spank him once and call him a bad boy, which I did: it's like those times in church when the last thing in the world you want to do is laugh, so you hold your breath or think tragic thoughts to keep from laughing. I had never spanked an old man before, especially one who wore a garter belt to keep in all that loose skin around his belly. I think he said he was fifty-eight but he was more like ten years older than that, with a pathetic loop of dyed black hair he combed across his forehead like a wet noodle. Such a dear, sweet old man. He took me out to dinner most every night and he played with Nathan and even rocked him to sleep with lullabies, and I didn't care what he looked like or how he smelled old and musty in the morning. He was good to me and that's all that mattered. He bought me dresses and told me I was the most beautiful woman in the world. And you know what? I felt like it, when I was with him. I knew I was beautiful, knew it so deeply I didn't even have to look in the mirror. But I knew it wouldn't last and sure enough, three months into it he went to jail for gambling. Seems he'd been there before because he went away real calm, like he'd been expecting it for weeks and what a relief, it was finally here. The thing about Charlie was that he didn't care how he came across or what people thought of him, how some might think him foolish for fawning all over me, a woman a third his age who's really small, and this made him lovable in a deep-down way. He just didn't care what people thought and that was turn-on enough for me, most nights. But he couldn't make me hot like Hank, no two ways about it, and to my everlasting shame and confusion I'm still physically attracted to the man who tried to kill me—the counselor even said that's normal.

What's normal about wanting to make love to a man who wants to take your head off?

My time at the shelter taught me a few things: that there are a lot of us out there, more than you can count, that our stories are mostly the same, that each of us is probably still secretly in love with the man that beat us, that maybe we even thought we deserved it somehow. We all thought we could change them, or that they would change by themselves. And sometimes, when I can't sleep, I go into Nathan's room to see if my baby has any of those violent tendencies, but all I see is my beautiful boy with that dark curly hair. I can almost hear him growing in the dark. I get tired worrying about what his life will be like—it's probably the most exhausting thing I know. Looking at him, wondering if he's like him. Could he be capable of dragging a woman down the stairs by her hair? No way, there's just no way. Because of the abuse it was touch and go if I could even have Nathan at all, but he was a baby determined to be born and he came out normal and screaming like the world was on fire.

The hardest part was when some young nurse started to cry when she saw all my bruises: what right did she have to do that, to embarrass me in front of those people at the hospital? I yelled at her for that and told her to get the hell out of my room until I became a mess myself, crying before I even had my baby.

Sometimes he approaches me in a dream and he's holding something behind his back. It's sunny outside, and one of his silver-capped teeth starts to gleam and then I wake up because I know he's going to kill me. Then it's the same routine: I rush into Nathan's bedroom to see if he's okay, go the bathroom and wash my face, and get back into bed, crying myself to sleep. It doesn't make sense, what he did to me—I can't figure it out. At the same time, no matter what anyone says, I know in a weird way that he loves me, even if he doesn't really know how to love. He loves me the only way he knows how, which is with slow deep-down loving when things are good, so that the middle of me is where he was always meant to be and he can be so gentle then, you would not even believe it: he's not the same man who hit me, and I would do anything for him, anything.

It pays to be matter-of-fact about these things.

Some nights he even took me out to play pool and loved to tell me how much he liked seeing me bend over and shoot the eight into a corner pocket and beat him. Beat him! Beat him! Do you hear? He only ever looked at me, never at any other woman, and he protected me from other men and got real jealous if I so much as strayed a few feet from his side. I grew used to that protectiveness and came to count on it. That's what they didn't understand, that he could also be so good to me, buying me lacy things and getting on his hands and knees to tell me how much he loved me, until he hugged my midsection and cried and said sorry, sorry, sorry, as if his heart would bust wide open. And even when I told him about Nathan he was so overcome with joy that he climbed the roof of our little shack and yelled how he was the happiest man in the world, with the prettiest wife ever and someday, someday soon, a son he could raise and take with him everywhere.

When a man like this hits you, you know somewhere deep inside yourself that he's also hitting himself, that for every blow he lands on you it's because he's scared and you hold a power over him that no one else does which makes him that crazy, to the point of wanting to kill you. I know it doesn't make sense but that's the whole truth of it, and neither the shelter or the beatings themselves ever tell the whole story. He's not completely evil and I'm not always abused. It's not either/or or but/and. Some nights in bed, when I want him near me so I can touch that hard warm back, I whisper his name and I know he's staring up at the ceiling somewhere and can hear me calling him and then, yes, I touch myself, but it's never the same, it's just not the same thing. We had it bad for each other and there was nothing in the world he wouldn't do to please me physically. The worst it got was when he wanted to have sex with me in my behind, and I even came to like that too: there wasn't nothing dirty about it, no matter what the preachers say. He told me he wanted to be everywhere I lived and felt, and I let him go there time and time again. There was nothing dirty about it. We used to do this when we knew we couldn't afford to get pregnant, and after a while I got used to it and even came to like it a whole lot. You would too, with a man like that. You wanted to know everything, so I'm telling you. I can't just tell you about the beatings, that wouldn't be fair—and I can't just tell you how sorry I am it didn't work out, that I had to run away in the middle of the night. At the shelter we had these feminist women, and their hair was really short, and some of them looked almost like men, though some were real pretty too, and they all were very kind to me. They'd gently recommend I read something, but I haven't read a book since fifth grade and Mrs. Clark read it out loud anyway. The name of the book was *Old Yeller*, and after she read it to us I thought, *If reading is that sad, who needs it?* But I'm not dumb. I know that. I try to cut down on watching TV because I heard it's not good for your brain. I could tell, though he never let on, that Charlie thought I was a little stupid—not a lot, but maybe a little. And when I knew he thought that it was almost worst than Hank beating me.

I'm not stupid.

I'm not stupid.

I was always taught that the thing you really gotta learn is how to chase boys and, once you catch one of them, how to hold onto one. I told that to one of the feminists down at the shelter and she smiled at me and said, "Now you have to learn how to chase yourself." I don't know what makes some people dedicate themselves to shelters like that, but I'm really glad they do. Now I have to think about what kinds of values I want Nathan to grow up with.

One afternoon I went to visit Charlie in jail for maybe a half-hour before he was sent off to prison, more cupcakes, I drove up our gravel road, which winds around some pine trees for about three hundred yards, to our little rented house way out in the middle of nowhere, and I just knew my baby wasn't inside. I knew it like you know that first drop of rain will be followed by a hush of sucked wind before the downpour begins and you know you're going to get soaked before it even starts to fall. I left Nathan at home because he was sleeping so peaceful-like and I would be right back. I was not in the habit of leaving him alone, ever, but this time I thought I'd make an exception because he was fighting naps lately and this time he was sucking his binkie way off in dreamland. He was asleep, he was asleep, I swear to you he was asleep. I'd be right back; I'd be back before he knew it. I knew he was gone the second I turned on to the road from the high-way. I felt his absence before I saw his empty crib and the crumpled sheets there. It was the only time I left him alone, the only time ever, I swear to you. Everything stopped inside me, clicked off, and my whole body felt drained until I thought I might drift off like a balloon. So he had found me after all this time, he had taken my baby, he was going to make me suffer bad for going away, for leaving him, for sending him to jail. I sat down for I don't know how long in the chair near Nathan's crib and thud, thud, thud. My life was over, if it even ever was; he would scrape out my insides with a spatula and tell me to eat them, and I would, I would do anything he told me now, he could have me any way he wanted, he could gut me like a fish. And I felt like a fish in that chair, my gills lifting and falling like fish gills do, like they were blades of grass lifted by a breeze where all the buffalo were killed, before winter but after the end of the world. He had Nathan. He had my baby. After a hundred years or maybe five minutes (I don't know) I got up from the chair and never in my whole life did I feel so calm: I took off my shoes, went into the kitchen, and took the longest knife from the wood block.

Well, finally, he would carve us out ourselves after I would try to carve him, he would cut into us with the point of this blade, and maybe even he would wear our ears and fingers around his neck. But he would not hurt me anymore and he would not ever touch Nathan ever again. I would make sure of that. I walked out onto the porch with the sun going down and the crickets screaming and I walked into the backyard and down the trail to where the Nemaha flows in threads like braided hair and I would find him there in a clearing with Nathan on his knee, pointing to the sky, and he would off us as slowly as he pleased, after I tried stabbing him in the neck and he would end up doing me any way he wanted, and Nathan and me would escape to heaven because heaven was wherever we were together and he was nowhere to be found. So I walked the trail and my feet started to bleed and I felt almost drunk and nothing really hurt me because I could not feel it anyway, and I wiped the tears away with the hem of my dress, because who cared now, and I thought about three pancakes I'd serve that very day to some unshaven trucker who hit on me, and thought how nice it would be to curl up between those pancakes with Nathan and just never wake up. I thought about my own mama and how she gave me a doll she'd had as a girl, stuffed with sawdust coming out and blond corn silk for hair, and how she said my dark auburn hair was ten times prettier, and thank you, Mama, thank you for saying that; and the receipts I had in my purse from Wal-Mart for Nathan's car set that he was just really starting to get into, and other voices came and went, *You can bet on this if you want*, said Charlie, and I think I'm tired now, so tired I dragged the knife like a sword, I let it droop at my side, you know how shadows fall on the far side of weeds and they are so much longer than the weeds.

When I got to the clearing I was ready to die; I was ready to see him grinning at me like he always did in bad dreams and in real life when he was setting up to punish me. But he wasn't there. He wasn't there. In a pool of sunlight, in light so bright and shining and clear you could almost see through anything, Nathan was chasing a little girl around in a circle and they were laughing; she was a beautiful girl with beautiful chestnut-colored hair and she had on a schoolgirl's uniform and the trees were full of their laughing. She was no girl I had ever seen; she would almost let Nathan catch her and then she'd run away. They made circles running after each other until I thought I knew how the earth turned and could feel it in my stomach, because this is how it was done between dawn and nightfall, and I knew the sunlight going down was burning bright in both them and me and always would. I sat down on a large rock and let the knife drop from between my hands and the blade of it was only sunlight now, cutting my face with flashed light. My baby was safe. My baby was safe. Fringed on the edge of the woods behind until you almost could not see him was a man who watched them play, a man with long black hair, perfectly still, so at first I thought he was a tree, but he was watching them play like I was watching them, both of us watching them run in circles.

I should have cried out, "You can catch her, Nathan! You can catch her!" but the words only came to me later when it made sense to think them. I started crying with relief and joy until all the water inside me came out and flowed into the Nemaha and all we did was watch them run and play, and I was so thankful and so relieved that I did not know what to do with myself, because I've never been much of a praying person, but still I knelt down, closed my eyes to the sounds of their playing, and prayed to God *Thank you for letting us be safe.*

The man came over to me and he brushed my hair and he smelled like polished stones baking in the sun, the cleanest smell I ever smelled, like the beginning of the ocean. And when I raised my head he looked like every picture of Jesus I had ever seen. Was I dreaming or was I already dead? I didn't know then and I don't know now. Nathan fell and started to cry then, and I quick kissed the man's hand, gathered up my skirt, and ran across the field. The girl in the school uniform was gone. It was only Nathan now, and he had wandered far away from home. I got to him, gathered him up in my arms, and almost squeezed the breath out of him. His crying filled the trees where before it was the laughter of kids playing. "Shhh, baby, sshhh, Mama's here," and eventually he quieted down. It was darker then, and kinda chilly. I looked around and the man and the girl were gone. Had they ever really been there in the first place? I carried my baby home the long two miles back, gathered up his things and teddy, dropped him off at my girl-friend Madeline's house, and went back to our place, where everything was still haunted by him. I knew I had to change somehow. I couldn't afford to be afraid anymore. I had to sit there awhile and get used to this new sense of things. I said it out loud on the front porch: "I am no longer afraid of you. I am no longer afraid of you. I am no longer afraid of you." I said it until I believed it, and then I went to Madeline's and picked up my son.

Joshua Tidbowl

Can't breathe in here, can't hardly breathe. Do me a favor and open the window just a crack, above your head. We're gonna have us a long talk and I can't start talking if I can't breathe. Wife Evelyn dead, only kid gone into the Marines. I live at the end of this road with my one lung, which I have studied on an X-ray machine: it is the one thing that has kept me breathing all these years. So I will tell you about the accident and how I saw him.

I lay in the middle of the highway at the end of July in 1967 in the year of Our Lord, outside Paducah, Kentucky, and death was coming for me over the fields like a light held so precious and hovering that each mote of dust was a world unto itself, disintegrating before me, drifting into brightness, and sheaves of waving grass hummed a sea-sound as I descended into the eyes of the moth and the buttercup before the cosmic thunderclap. I was dead to rights, dead, but somehow hanging on to the whining of a distant mosquito coming ever closer. Sound was my only salvation then. When that mosquito reached my face, where I couldn't swat it with my broken hand, it would be over.

I saw a blackbird fly above and could make out the shaft of grain it carried in its beak, frayed from being blown about like the hair of a lover thrashed in the throes of love, and the bird's eye that held the world curved at the edges so that everything was curved and nothing was straight and this was how time worked, warped and peeling back. I was the aperture of a hidden eye suddenly opening, the great gaping yawn of the world, where so much collapses under the weight of its own unfolding, a wooden hoop of fire in my granddaddy's backyard which he pushed with a stick to pogo down the yard as he whooped and hollered and yelled, "There's your rim of fire, boy!" and lusted for country girls in lofts of shining hay, where you could jimmy yourself into flesh in hot bolts of ecstasy—"Come on then, Come on"—small hatreds, pettiness, prayers I knew were false: none of it mattered, all of it went into the making and breaking of worlds.

The sound of steam, and soon I heard a moan come from the other wreck like a sigh from a man of metal born until he was not man but moan, leaking away into the twilight of his sound, just a few notes away from dying, just a little while now, won't be long now, a doomed moan with maybe one creaking vowel left inside him, calling down the sound-altar of the world before it was made acceptable to Him, and then the moaning ceased, Lord be praised, letting the lighted fields take him without further cause.

You know America is just one big car wreck, don't you? You know it's vehicular homicide, with folks playin' their country music of Patsy Cline or what the young coloreds like to play today (Shoot the police, Shoot the police)? You know America is on a collision course with itself, that the bigger those fancy leisure trucks get—guzzle, guzzle—are just setting up to make off with your soul and plain raise hell? Some people—it is true—face death with an open mouth and you see their spittal gleaming like gossamer rays. Some let it take them perfectly still, as if they were moss on a burnished stone, getting a preview of the eternal nothingness that awaits them. I waited in the latter with a nice chunk of the highway lodged in my cheek.

And you want to know why he visited me, what I have to say about it, I know you done think it, so don't turn red and say it ain't so; antlers on my walls, things you don't approve of, that embarrass you for my

IG-norance, my nonsensical ways, my squint-eyed obsessions, because I choose to live here and read Horace in Latin and you just can't accept the contradictions, can you, that he visits trash, because that's where he came from, how he talks and listens, how he beckons for a beer, loops his ponytail over one shoulder and ties it with a red rubber band, and hee-haw, hee-haw, it's revenge of the rednecks or at least acknowledgment that we are alive, and what the hell are you going to do about it, huh? I don't know the answer either, if that gives you any comfort. I live in a mud-hut with no running water and I speak in tongues. That chair you're sitting in is mystically charged, even if the arm is loose. My name is Joshua Tidbowl and I'm the one who called him the Mover of Bones because he found her and dug her up and now he's on a spree, spreading God's word through the musical cadence of her expired spirit, which is restless, restless, due to the violent manner of her death—and a whole nation's obsession with someone who can't be found. Outrage! cries the land. Bring down the locusts and let the frogs roar like lions!

It began in a stream, in a thread of clear water. It began with the simple word "No": I will not let you defile me, I will not let you touch me like that, though she did not have the words. He took scissors to her clothes first, he cut expertly into her school-girl uniform to expose certain parts of flesh to look at, where he trembled like jelly in a fire. Then plaid designs offset fields of snow, with here and there a birthmark to make his blood run hotter. He cut off her school-girl dress square by square, rectangle by rectangle, this way and that, as she laid tied up and squirming beneath, just a girl. Not a dolphin, mind you, subject to crying out for her ma and pa, crying out for the light, for the un-darkness and her own dolls, which she dressed prim and proper because somewhere out there in doll-land a suitor was waiting to make her doll a tea-setting kind of home, where no one did anything and everyone was good. Now you know the evil part of geometry: he cut her into shapes he could awe over before he did anything else, before he even violated her body.

Before long her clothes were systematically cut off her to expose that white flesh no man had ever touched, and he savored each design he cut, like shards of chipped light. He cut her down to nakedness piece by piece, the whole ritual protracted to a point where he could not live without those clothes, so he put them in a cigar box and tied it with a ribbon, where he would later rearrange the scraps into the uniform of the dead girl on his bed and spread his own seed in his hand; locks of her hair, a toenail he pared off and prayed to, even a totem of her knuckle would serve him later on, and now you see how cutting straight lines is evil, don't you, even if you're mowing your yard. See how they become the implements of a force that wants only to control—not to liberate—the roundness therein, boundaries of desire.

But God does not work in lines; no, he works in roundness, like water moving over stones, or he uses lines to expose the folly of man's waste. And that's where her voice got started: just No, then. No, no. Which is what God will say to you if you ask for something your soul don't need. No, pilgrim, no. No is God's way of saying, emphatically and forever, I love you, child, into whose clay nostrils I first blew breath. No to the quickness of your blood. No to the hands that would touch me that way, no to the fantasy he sought to live out, because she was not a Thing to which his manhood grew hard and bone-warped like a spoon. She was real, is real, and her realness was not in any budding pubic hair but a voice which first said No to him, a word that even as he tortured her he did not understand: "What do you mean no? Whence comes this no, no, no, no, no?" He knew the no would come at first but he did not know it would gather in strength and beauty so that even while he did what he did, cut her up into all those little pieces, his wickedness was presided over by a spirit that watched them. Already her hymn was beginning in that place beyond walking down a dusty road, rising above, the opening parts of which you will hear when you depart this earth for a better place; heaven is that place where your name can be sung as part of His eternal hymn. And it was this hymn, given her by God because she had the dignity of a no to his jack-in-the-box evil, that kept jumping out in hydra-headed wonder. He made love to her dismembered leg, but was a fool for doing it, a desperate and sick fool mocked for all eternity for his perversions, and even that was risen out of the darkness to become her voice, bending his wicked practice to a sound he could not defile, much less answer or contain, because it rendered him into a gaping, eyeless fish with a panoply of flies. No, that precious, beautiful word in the mouth of a little girl pulverized his wickedness into a pocketful of dust you could put in a sandcastle and bury in the grace of God's sand. Evil moves fast because it is threatened with extinction. But this is what you have to know, what to hear: No flowered into death, then, as all negation does, that void into which you will commend your spirit to be summoned by a ray of light you cannot see. And that's when the stream began, the stream of her agony becoming a voice singing, and after awhile, after he had his fun with her body (believe me, the aftertaste of his affair took away all the pleasure hitherto), her cries became a beautiful song, had to be, not unlike that brook where children play and deer leap and trout shimmer like a thousand rainbows at once—you know the one I mean even if you ain't been there—and before God you become the child you were always meant to be and your sins are washed away and whatever bad thoughts afflicting you, or even tattoos, disappear and you become not new but what you always were before you came out of your mama, "trailing clouds of glory." That song, that stream coming out of her dead mouth. Gimme some of that, though it is a tough road to hoe; let me crawl over slag heaps of glassy obsidian cutting into my legs. I will cut myself for what I always am before I ever was. *Was, was.* No, sir, and again no, sir, I deign not to be touched like that.

That's why Breedlove had to dig up her body. He dug her up because she lived the only life worth living and she died the only death worth dying, preserving her integrity. Her bones had to go on a rock-'n-roll tour; they had to be excavated so that others could feel the shock of her purity.

Don't you see it, child, don't you see?

You come here for answers but you don't even know what you stumbled into, do you? How it could change your life because you're living the wrong one now. Else, why are you here? Lest you have everything in the world and even then (though the world is not your home, you need to understand that), at some shining point you're gonna want what she had, it's the only thing *to* want, and you would dig up her body and she would talk to you and you would talk to her and you would both agree we are not long for this world and that's a good thing if you live it right, die it right; you will be that boy or girl or dog's spirit that never knew any home except the small voice that comes but once or twice in a lifetime. And if it says "dig up a girl's body and turn into Jesus Christ" then you dig up a girl's—body which is lattice-like anyway—and you become the Son of God.

So when I lay in the middle of a country highway with a truck on my neck, my teeth sharpening themselves on the hot cement till I could cut through rawhide just by smiling, I saw the man you speak of twenty miles away walking toward me in shimmering heat waves, because if you can't judge distance what good are you? I was a pebble at the bottom of a stream looking up through cold water to see the flickering God-figure coming toward me, a witness to the dumb anguish of one of his creatures in pain. I was part truck then, part seeing stone; I knew the other fella was dead. His last moan issued out of him like farting oak board, no way to go, no way to go. If you coulda riveted my eyes to the bolts of a jet airplane I could not have been more steadfast nor so intent; he was moving into the compass of my heart in the shape of a gathering dust storm, and once he got to the center of it I would be delivered up for good.

It was then I knew a man or woman must come to terms with his own foolishness if he hopes to understand why he is here; he must go back to the rough conditions of his birth and reconstruct the folly of a life avoiding God, though only God can give him the moments of being truly alive. I avoided Him because I knew the price would be dear for following Him (His light crowded me into dark spaces; like an infant I crouched in the dark, sucking my toes and fingers), for proclaiming what I knew, because to know at all is to harbor deep inside yourself the lightning bolts of insurrection which cannot know what they strike at until they hit and whop, shazam, you are fried and your wig flies off; for when they do I say again, "Ah, God, you are electrified and charged in a different atmosphere with horse-teeth in your mouth and will drop that purse or wallet until finally you say, "I can't do it anymore." Pretend I don't know what I know, can't live the wicked life that gauges itself by the rising and falling of erectile flesh. The knowledge is like a Bo weevil burrowing inside your brain; it's like a fat lip you can't hide, and it will take whatever shape God abides and hunt you down like a rabbit.

You ask how a man can be born of metal, how he can come out of a contraption designed and tuned by his own hand, and I do not know, I do not know. All I know was, I was born again at the end of my life, and what had I done up till then to merit such violent and devastating grace? Why was prophecy laid down upon my tongue like a sprinkling of glowing salt? Was it because my left lung was becoming an empty sack in my chest? Was it the gravel taste of the highway that henceforth I would link in my mind with the harsh necessity of His love? A fatal accident is a strange place to wake up and more American than baseball. But the story has no beginning or end, no cause and sequence, because He don't work that way; instead He rolls about like a divine boulder to rupture the fabric of time when he sees fit, to punch through that white muslin sheet you are all wrapped up in and say, "I did not ask for this," and He touches you anyway and everything is changed. So he came for me out of the hovering dust of summer and touched my tongue. Even if I lived just one more second I was saved because one year to him is an instant, and a whole lifetime a mere eyelash and blink.

I saw the highway for what it was: not a conveyance merely for commerce and traffic and getting away, but the stone river of his mercy, where He takes so many of His children to be washed. I drove out that day as so many do and have, on the pretense of some errand between one county and the next—maybe it was a basket of oranges, maybe I had to get Evelyn something from town—but the real reason was that I was lost and restless and seeking to find what had been missing from my life. If you watch most folks behind the wheel you will see they really are ghosts doing a boogie dance down the highway, wishing they had some kind of other ulterior form, maybe something with wings; you will see the emptiness of our plight on earth if you are honest with what you see, driving behind the wheel. And behind the wheel you will hear that haunting refrain that echoes in closed lips, something about "I wish, I don't know, I am lost, why did I do that, who am I, what time is it in my heart, why do I think about that childhood tree that keeps calling out to me in scraped whispers of a thousand leaves?" You will see them as God sees them, and want to take each of them close into your bosom and rock them back and forth and tell them in a quiet, calm voice, "I will lead you all the way home," and brush their foreheads with your lips. You will be so tall then, and the highway, any highway at all, even a back dirt road in the country, will traipse its way around your hidden inmost self like silk spinning out of a worm, and you will see how love works then, how it truly is a winding path that has no speed limit and chooses how you will die and in what weather. That's why he took her on the road in America and that's why his Father chose the road as his one true church, and you can only hope He will hit you at the speed of light and obliterate your creeping, crawling animal fear. Roadkill's divine in His hands. And there's no preaching to be done after this, no, I told you so, no sighting of UFOs (though His light is an orb that can devastate the land): just you and the witnessing, and maybe your blood running away in the dust.

Who hath been touched by the Mover of Bones has seen a great light and will carry it before them in their mouths until the sense of the world dissolves and the real one comes out, the one where the Christ Child is a glowing parachute or cloud come to envelope you; he who hath touched or seen the dead girl's bones will know what singing is, and you will find this witness looking to the end of his allotted time to meet his maker with the brine of repentance on his lips. Oh, do not disbelieve the Mover of Bones, the Mover of Bones who shows how what is left of her skeleton bones do the celestial dance around the seven candlesticks in the middle of His chest and the seven angels with trumpets in their mouths. Oh, move your bones, child, move them where He wills it: move them into snowfields, into deserts, plains, and mountains, past cities where the smog hangs like clouds, into caves where strange men live and gnaw on stalactites of bitter salt. These too are prophets and have foreseen His coming in the package of a dead girl who said "No," who halfway into her own dismemberment rose into a hymn. Was His own death chamber not vacant soon after? Did not they who witnessed from afar the slow death of His son not also move His sacred bones down from Golgotha—and did not his own mother weep at the sight of His dead body?

Are not we all, every one of us, called to move the bones of those we love and those we despise?

Oh, I say again, move those bones, child, move what skeletons come your way, even if you have to swim in the dirt and eat your way toward them; move them up to the Lord, hold them in your arms, say you are sorry for ever letting them go. Put them on the mantel over the fireplace and ask the bones to talk to you, and then you will find they are a Confederate soldier with Dixie on his mind, a black slave who crouched in the swamp, ate rats, and had the courage of steel; so many bones and spirits you cannot number them.

And where now do you think they are headed? Do you think the janitor and his frail bundle of singing bones will run forever? I say unto you, dark days are ahead if you do not welcome them. Do not turn away the Mover of Bones; do not betray him; do not doubt the validity of his purpose. The dead girl and the janitor have suffered enough. As the Father has bidden, so I bid you.

Missy Sanders, One of the Lost

The people you leave behind pick you out of crowds at movie theaters and checkout lines and other busy places, across street corners before the light turns green and people hurry in front of them; they look down alleys and up at the roofs of buildings where you couldn't be, but that's the part of them that keeps looking, keeps trying to make you appear wherever they look, because they'll never be at peace until they find you. They tell themselves, *There she is, there she is,* only it's not you, just someone who looks like you. And there are so many girls who have my hair color and lanky frame—and they have to let go all over again, each time they think they see you, and this is the thing that keeps hurting them and won't let up, that keeps threatening to break them wide open all over again, so that wherever you are you want to tell them, "Stop, please just stop. Let me go." Because they can't get enough of you when you're gone, they're frantic with their arms and fingers and want to cover you with their sobs in the middle of the night. Then where is the smell of death coming from? It's coming from you, that's where.

You don't have to feel sorry for me. You don't have to cry. All those tears just end up in the sea anyway. You don't have to imagine how I died (though you can't help it) or see me back into some kind of memory or scenario where I never was, not the way you see it anyway, me buying a skirt, me being a smart ass to my parents and getting grounded. My first kiss, my first period. The way my training bra chafed across my chest. Or how I couldn't stop shuddering one night when I was four and my mother thought I had a fever only it was the night, the thing I saw that would happen to me coming from far away. There's nothing for you to imagine except your own fears and fantasies, the things that will never be true. Feel something else. What I want now is some kind of tenderness for other living things, a kind of acceptance before I go away. It doesn't have to be a lot. Start with a bird or a tree, then move on to people.

People are the hardest. Look at their hands, see how they hold things. Because being sorry has nothing to do with me or any of us who are lost. Neither does pity. Neither does outrage. Now is the time for a special kind of courage you don't see much, the courage to love the person who hates you and wants you dead. I can't get this through to my parents. They're clinging to what I used to be, before he raped and killed me, not who I am now. I try to tell them. I try to let them know in my own special way. But the living are strange, their minds work overtime, they think that sad craziness is the only way to react, and it goes through them like a sickness. But the wind passes over everything and sometimes you have to let go so that the light from far away can come back and live inside you.

When you pass over to the other side it's like moving to a house where there are no walls and the sun is always shining, like a house made of fear turning into a house of love, and you see that time has nothing to do with what's real. Even when you walked the earth the best part of you knew this, like a deep down secret hurt you couldn't share with anyone. So you leave behind time and you leave behind sorrow like a watch on the table with the second hand going round and round, ticking, but it's a hollow threat and always has been, and that's what you learn when you go back to the light. There's nothing to be afraid of anymore. The part of you that's wise and loving never leaves and never goes away, even if you were just fifteen when you were killed, like the light shining on a cool autumn day through the trees so that the leaves are filled only with this brightness.

He had a scar on his knuckle shaped like a campfire. It was white like the fat on a chicken. He said a voice told him to do it and I believed him, and if the voice was that loud then I guess you have to listen to it no matter what it says. But I told him he didn't have to, I begged him not to, but the other voice was louder and commanded him and so he did it and I became very quiet. The body is a temple where the light lives, I learned that as a little girl. If you saw how he lived there you would shudder with joy and nothing, not even a man with a knife, could ever hurt you, because no matter how far down he cut or carved you up with his anger and pain, the light lives in a place that's quiet and peaceful, where it holds everything and asks you to come and sit by its side. When I talk to my parents and the people who miss me I talk to them in the discarded things of the world, a page torn out of a phonebook, scraps of litter blowing in the wind, a trash bag pinned up in a tree. But they do not hear me and they do not see me. Their eyes have gone dark because of the sorrow and all they can see is how I used to be, the photograph they put up when I was missing. If I could show them how much I love them and how much their love means to me, they could not hear it with human ears or see it with their eyes, but I stand in the middle of their suffering anyway and they do not know that I am there.

When I was in my agony God showed me the deep dark sockets of His wounds while the man killed me; he held up his palms for me to see and I looked through them to the other side where there was nothing but sky and more sky forever. I could see the blood flowing out from his side in a stream that rose to the surface of the table. I saw that the shape of his wounds was like the heads of newborns coming out of their mothers and almonds that people put in their mouths on a hot summer day, because the pain and the suffering are part of the beauty and there is no other way than this, and I know that now. I turned my dead eyes up to a corner of the ceiling and saw a clear white drop of water where the light seeps in. I kept my eyes on the light, which was different from any other light I had ever seen, brighter and fuller; it kept getting bigger, like the coming of a new world.

I looked at the killer and saw that his face was made of dark wood teeming with termites, that he was made like a wall and the termites gave him brain and mouth and the smell of meat on his breath; the walls of his body were too high to see over. He smelled like gasoline and cigarettes and he wanted to get rid of me when he was done, so he took me out of the basement of his house in a bag and put me in the trunk of his car. He was gentle with me then, laying me down as if I might break. He drove for a long time. I was still bleeding and not yet dead but he did not know this. I said in the darkness, in the wound, "I can't see anything," and dark silence answered me. The blood was rich like wine, like my blood. I did not think of anything or fear anything or wonder where I would be; just the dark silence and nothing. The dark of the trunk and nothing. The lake of my blood where I lay, at the bottom of it. The dark getting darker until nothing was all around me and I felt the blank darkness cradle me like a seed planted in the ground. And then nothing. Nothing except the wound, which I became aware of in the dark.

When I was a little girl I used to hear a cricket under the porch, but the cricket was always hidden, and it knew when storms were coming and lightning and the long twilight of summers where it lived, sounding from its sliver under the porch, sounding in the planks of the porch and the weeds and the delicate puff of the spider web. I listened to the cricket, one of my favorite things in the world. I would sit on the porch with my bare feet dangling over the rails and think of the cricket somewhere beneath me, alert to things coming and going, singing from its hiding place. And hush now, there's no need to talk. Not in the dark silence, not even ever. It's okay. It's okay. It's okay. You know what dark silence is now and it's nothing to be afraid of because there's nothing more he can do and you are released from the pain and the fear and the dark, just the dark, and the silence that wraps around it. Can you hear the cricket? Can you remember it? You think of the sound always. You're ready for God's hand now, he wants to show you how he suffered. The cricket sang when you were little because you became a part

of the porch, the part it knew about and did not mind, the part listening in the dark like a long blade of grass or a drop of rain. You saw the
dark coming and the night rain and if you could go back now it would
be in the sound of the cricket and nothing else, for the peace you felt
and the way the darkness came over you like air, like wind, like nothing before or since, as you enter the wounds of the Lord. It's okay, the
dark: darker than you've ever known it could be, dark like the end of
the cricket sounding under the porch, the time you heard nothing, saw
nothing beyond the porch, because it was darkness falling.

Missy, are you coming in?
I'll be right in, I promise.

But instead you stayed outside, you stayed there; the darkness had
not yet reached the bottom of your feet to fill up your whole body. And
soon after you didn't want to know where the cricket was or what it
looked like because it was waiting in the dark for something to come
and take it away, the sound of footsteps, the sound of silence, passing
cars, bird calls, screen doors closing, wind in the trees, senses you could
not make sense of. For someone to come and take the cricket away,
your one joy, your secret pleasure, what no one could take away from
your ears. To know as a girl that God's dark wounds were coming for
you where they drove in the nail. To be a part only of that, to know it
like the darkness of the trunk where he was taking you, and the fields
beyond where he burned and buried you next to the gnarled roots
of a sycamore tree. In the dark I dreamed of other darknesses, other
faint and distant places, where a part of me had always lived in twilight
cricket sounds, in the one memory that no blade could cut away. I was
inside God's hand where the nail went through and the hollow space
was like wave after wave of love's opening, peeling back against the
light until I could not see how far the wound went because it went on
forever; you pass through and you pass through and you wait in the
endless dark for him to take you out into the light.

Missy? Missy? We're looking for you, Missy. How long
must we suffer?

He took me out to a far away place in the woods where the branches of bare trees rubbed against each other and sighed, and when he opened the trunk the tide of my blood flowed over the side and splashed his feet. He got sick in the grass. I was ready to meet the Lord because I had lived a part of his suffering, in the wound of his hand as it washed my soul clean. I saw my body from above as one would see an island hacked and charred by warring men, and among the devastation and the waste I saw that my skin was white like alabaster and the other was crying and weeping and blamed me for making him do it, accusing me while another half of his self told him to be quiet and to finish what he had started, while still another called him names before it too broke down in a garble of hissing voices. Then silence. Then nothing again except for the friction of branches. I was high above my body and heard the cawing of a crow at the top of the sycamore tree. I wanted to stroke his hair but I did not because he took away my lifeless hands. He doused my body with gasoline and lit it on fire and threw me into a dark pit. My bones sang like violins but he could not hear them. I passed through the wounds of the Lord on my way to heaven. They connected east and west, north and south, and every place that stretched out like his arms on the cross. There was nothing that did not pass through his suffering on the way to his love and the distant glow at the end of it. Points of light dazzled me on the way so that I felt I was dying all over again and could not see for the blindness. Then I saw his swollen and beaten face like an apple rotting in the sun, his crown of thorns, sharp worms burrowing into his head. How, Lord, but there were no words to describe it. He showed me seeds and took me into a flower bud. He showed me milk in the veins of a baby, how wind takes the rain and makes a sheet of it, and how the oceans subside over the scales of a starfish. I was not dead-dead, just a small part of the light, a dust mote looking for its blindness. No one could hurt me in this love, and my suffering was only a part of the one who had made me, the one who had died on a cross. Nothing was lost, though they said I was missing and could not be found; nothing was not anything you could imagine because I was no longer here but everywhere, their grief for me could not go on because they carried the darkness of their ignorance like straw in their mouths.

The ones I left behind are searching for their car keys. They're fumbling for their lighters and swearing because they can't light the cigarette fast enough with their trembling fingers. They're stopped in traffic, seeing me where I am not, the ghost of hair length and hair color in another girl that used to be mine, the lanky limbs I was still growing into, the horse smiling of my toothy smile. Missy, Missy, is that you? I say to them quietly "I am here, I am here." I am right in front of you, I am inside of you forever. But they can't hear that yet; their ears are full of a dull static moan that keeps them from hearing me. Here I am. Over here. In this wind-blown leaf, in the call of a mourning dove. Here. I am right here though you cannot touch me and you cannot see me. I won't ever leave you. Only you can't have me back the way I was, the girl I used to be. It doesn't work that way. I am not losing you, I am not ready to lose you. Close your eyes and be still. Close your eyes and don't say anything. Hush now. There. I am not lost. I am here. I am almost here.

Marian Keyes Wanders into the Night

I walked out barefoot, half-dressed, in the middle of the night with the door swinging wide until the springs sprained their elbows and him saying, "It ain't what it look like," grabbing at my arm, but it was: a giant hole tore open inside of me and it was over just like that and I started crying so hard I thought I'd never stop, wandering down the porch steps onto 24th at three a.m. with the gangs and the junkies cruising the dark like broken bottles held up to your throat. And I didn't care who or what saw me, me dragging my crying eyes in front of me like a skinny black dog with hardly any clothes on, the world teetering until I almost fell off it.

I came into the house after Tonya dropped me off from the home and I walked up the stairs and knew right away something was wrong because even the walls seemed to listen, and then I heard it upstairs, behind the door, and the pictures started to form in my head, "Mmm, that's right, uh-huh" moaning, doing the things we used to do because we knew the spots no one else could touch. I knew before I saw them, before I even opened the door: my baby done fool me all these years. It wasn't the act itself, but the other man's head bobbing up and down in a funky rhythm I had never seen before, like he was sucking on a vine that grew out of the ground until the whole tree was sucked into his mouth and not my man, the father of my baby. I opened my mouth and the cry came out bigger than the house, eating up the moon, and my sides felt like they do after hanging out with Donna and Rochelle, cleared out and aching from laughing so hard, but it was no laugh this time, just a cry I always knew was waiting somewhere deep inside of me even if I couldn't say what it was. And now I had to worry about AIDS and all kinds of shit I never even dreamed of but that would come later because I knew this wasn't the only one or ever would be: he would just keep going, being with other men, and it was like I didn't have eyes until I saw this, until I knew my life with him was a lie we kept telling each other.

I was just so tired of this kind of life, working at the home every night, cleaning and scrubbing and tending to the old folks, worrying about Jamal, who keeps staying out later and later until some nights he don't even come home. "Where you been?" I ask him. "What you get yourself into? Don't roll your eyes at me, boy, I'll knock them out of your head." But he never answers me; he won't let me into his life because he's seventeen and won't listen to his mama, even when I threaten him, even when I beg him to be safe. He just shakes his nappy head and tells me not to worry, that someday he's gonna take care of me, and then he puts those long skinny arms around me until I stop, I just stop, and almost quit breathing. I never knew such tiredness could take up so much room in one body, like it was kicking me out and slamming the door. The tiredness puts on its clothes, the tiredness goes to the home and works in a office four days a week. There ain't any me left.

If you are a black woman you wander out into the night and there ain't no difference between what you left behind and what's in front of you because you can't see, and that don't have nothin' to do with justice anyway. You walk out into the dark and hold onto empty pockets, turning them inside out, into the humid air and the screaming of sirens. The cry that come up out of me was a dark rainbow moving the furniture and bending the windows until they weren't glass anymore, but a secret flood carrying the stains of old mattresses and the hornet's nest he said he'd knock down but never did, and nothing was the same again. In the office once they asked me why my nails were so long and painted red, how could I pick up envelopes and all, and what I thought but did not say was, *I need 'em to pick out your eyes when you ain't lookin'.*

I left the house. I pulled my sweater tight around me and then I took it off and threw it away. He called after me from the porch, pulling at his pants. I kept touching my throat when the sobs came and my neck felt like a tennis racket, and I didn't care what I stepped on and the streetlights bleeded white, and everything was white, the whole world was white, but I was dark like the night and so I was invisible, even to myself. A thin chord pulled me out of myself and it was like someone telling me what to do, what to think, how to look for the end that is always coming. I wandered into the night. I smelled something dead in the alley and the funk of cheap cherry wine, trash in the gutters. I wandered into the night and became the night itself, and saw myself in a cracked drugstore window, the crack running down the center of my face where it always been, and so this is who I am, a wide-eyed frog with no flippers on its feet, divided down the center of my head. I am ugly and maybe that's why he let other men suck him. When you catch yourself in a mirror, what you see is a scared animal with no wits left inside its head crying when there's no one around to help, like a razor cutting you up, adding power to the mirror, that can only give you what you are and what you ain't. I hate mirrors, hate them for what they have to show me.

I came to the edge of a parking lot where there were no cars but weeds grow out of the asphalt like caterpillars, weeds with hooks and fingers sharp enough to climb up the sides of anything not quick enough to get away. They climb all over you if you stand there long enough, with viney hairs combing down the sides of an abandoned store, like sideburns saying "Hey baby." Shopping carts sat on their sides with their wheels in the air and I thought of Jamal's mouth and his first braces and how when he smiled it was like every fish in the world jumping from the water into the sun, and if I could just hold him there maybe he would not put himself in danger, but he was already getting away from me even then, listening to the sidewalks and something deep down in his own blood, until my voice became like the flutter of a bird he could just ignore and shoo away. Every parking lot is the same, especially at night, like no car ain't ever parked there and no one ain't ever walked across it, so why do they call it a lot when there ain't any and you have to use moon rocks to buy your clothes? I sat down and held my hands in my lap, rocking back and forth, bubbles coming from my mouth.

I bought Jamal's baby clothes down the street at K-Mart. I sang him to sleep each night in a low hum I made just for him. I took the blanket and tucked it up to his chin, and he used his chin to move the blanket down. His forehead shined with baby oil. I nursed him by switching him from one breast to the other, and we both wrung out then and ready for sleep. I lay him down in the dark. The breeze come in softly over the crib, like a piece of cotton dipped in hope. I didn't know there could be such peace; I didn't know it could arch over my tiredness and give it cause; I didn't know those moments were already moving away when the peace was there. I love my baby. He thinks being a man is never backing down to no one, ever, not even me; he thinks being a man is some kind of salt he can't let no one taste; he thinks he has to walk through plate glass windows and never flinch, that he has to cast his seed far and wide and keep going until somebody stronger than him stops him or till the police surround him on all sides with bright lights and pulled guns, telling him to put his hands up. And this is why he dropped out of school, stays out all night, looks cross-eyed at any kind of hope or authority, lives for today because there ain't no tomorrow. He sees what's all around him, some days getting worse and some better, but mostly the same, that we can't get out from under the shadow of this rock because we is shadows ourselves but it don't have nothing to do with it, I mean the color or whatever shade of gray. The world is a fucked-up place. It's fucked-up here and it's fucked-up all over, and I told him not to cuss, but I said it that night, over and over, "Lord, the motherfucker sucking on a man not my man no more, Jamal, baby, your mama so far out you can't keep track of her, no mama now just cryin', Lord, the motherfucker"—

And heat, what you do with that, the heat I had in the parking lot, crying on a curb and watching how the parking lot swayed in the dark like a cracked plate no one would eat off of, serving up its meal of dirt with no crumb-eaters around. I sat in the parking lot for I don't know how long, and then got up and started walking someplace else. For a second I thought I'd throw myself off a bridge, but we don't have no bridge tall enough for that round here, and that started me laughin', laughin' at my fool self because I'd have to borrow a bridge to do it.

I started laughing in the parking lot, me and the ghost cars going, whooping it up under the stars, and the night felt like a skin on my skin, not his skin but maybe someone else's, maybe even a woman's. Maybe his man and me just love the same thing, and that was funny too. I got up and walked across the train tracks. I stopped laughing and started crying again, laughter turning into water so fast you could almost touch where the two met and swapped emotions. And the gibberish hours, the hours of wandering alone, I knew that every watch was false and always would be and that I told time not by watching the moon or the streetlights flashing hellos and good-byes or any of the other signs you live by in the big bad city, but by the steps you take out on the very edge of everything alone, that's where real time lives and that's why folks go crazy. Jamal would learn that the hard way, and who says mothers want their children to learn, I do not want him to learn this lesson because he might not recover. I felt the night wrap around me like outer space.

I walked across an intersection where the houses on all four sides were boarded up. And there he was:

"You all right?"

"What?"

"Are you all right?"

"Say again."

"Are you all right? Are you hurt? Did you have an accident?"

I looked at him and I don't know where he come from: a long-haired white man in a beat-up truck sticking his head out the window in a bad part of town in the middle of the night. He come out of nowhere;

I so busy crying and laughing about the goddamned bridge that wasn't there that I didn't notice him stopped at the intersection.

"Do you need some help?"

You the one who lost, brutha; you the one out of the picture here. You way out of your league. But I did not say that.

"I'm wandering around and he-he . . ."

Tears. Sobs. Useless shit. Crying. Laughing. Moan. He—

"I can take you somewhere if you want me to."

Why would I get in some white man's truck? Why would I open myself up to that kind of trouble? But I did. I got in 'cuz I had no other place to go and I didn't give a fuck, either. I got in and we drove around awhile, me not sayin' nothin' and him just as quiet. I don't even know why he stopped for me or why he was in that part of town. I don't think he did, either, just two lost souls driving around an inner city waste—and I could see now why we do what we do, Jamal running so fast into manhood he jump out of his own shoes into other shoes too big for him but still running, running, running that maybe he would jump out of those shoes and come back to me a better man who just survived, survived. I want my baby to survive, I want him to thrive, I want him to live. And he nodded and just said "I know, I know."

"What you know of miracles?"

"How big are they on your list of priorities?"

After awhile he told me his name was Jesse, and we drove around for a few hours. Even though it was dark the dark did not reach so far inside me and the bridge I was thinking of became a toll bridge, no bridge at all, just a footstool to put in a light bulb or something like that. I started pointing things out to him: that's where I used to live, and that's where my daddy died, and you don't want to go in there. I didn't think about Russell back at the house; I didn't think of that other man's mouth on him. And Jamal was just a boy playing a man somewhere. Jesse said that even white boys in the suburbs stay out all night. But, Jesse, honey, they ain't hunting down the night till somebody's shot or in jail. He said he'll be all right, and I believed him; he was all I had just then. I wanted to believe him and he wanted to be believed, and I guess that's the beginning of hope anyway, a tiny seed you hold real careful in the palm of your hand. "He'll be all right," he said.

And I believed him because he come out of nowhere and that's where angels come from, nowhere you can't see or touch; I believed him. I believed him so much. I reached over and took his hand. He let me. It was a heavy and strong hand, and its warmth grew into me till I covered it with tears. Each time he said "It's gonna be all right, all right," something lifted from me, some kind of heaviness the night put on, that makes you shudder when you think you might turn into a bird. He drove me round the city and it was different inside his truck, like an aquarium at the zoo where the sharks cruise by your head but do not see you. We just two people shooting the shit and talking about our lives, and why certain things have to do us the way they do. He was a good man to ast me like that, and I wanted to do something good to him in return. All I had was my body. I never done it with no white man before, but I wanted to then.

Jamal, baby, you right to be restless, but I didn't put the restlessness there; it was the streets where you were never supposed to be. I know you think you belong to them and maybe you even think they calling down a hallway like a voice without a sound—"Come out and be a man"—but the only thing that works is to walk tall and stare straight ahead and hum something, sweet pea, hum a tune that will block out the voices of the street, because whatever myth you think you a part of is a bloody myth, not my baby who used to collect bottle caps and tell me someday you gonna buy me a five-foot chocolate cake and every day would be my birthday, the one before you was born. Jamal, baby, son, please come home: don't keep breaking my heart.

I said these words to the night, and he heard me. He didn't say nothin' after that. He didn't have to. I ast him to pull over in some dark place and we fell into each other's arms. He didn't give me no advice. I didn't ask him to. Just a brief hugging together because we was lonely and just had that moment. He looked at me and then he said, "You're gonna get through this; you're gonna be all right. And Jamal, he's gonna be all right too." I believed him; I squeezed his hand and I believed him. And later he dropped me off down at the corner.

I walked up the long porch steps that need a new coat of paint and when I looked back he was already gone. I looked off after him for a few seconds, and then I took my tired bones and my tiny seed of hope back into my home. Then he become who he had to be, his picture all over the papers because of what he did or didn't do, nobody can say for sure. He didn't do nothin' to me but love me for a few hours. No, he didn't do nothin' to me but help me get through the night my life changed forever.

Ed Jakowski

I help Mattie into the van. She's like a long stringy noodle in my arms, and she always gets slobber on my shoulder. She weighs maybe eighty pounds. "Up you go, Mattie," and I buckle her into the specially designed backseat in the van, the one I busted my ass to pay for. It has a mini built-in elevator and special handles and a cup designed for Mattie's hand I can strap around her wrist. She looks pretty snug in there, like an astronaut before liftoff. I haven't figured out yet how to keep her head from flopping from side to side, but I'm working on it.

What is your own daughter if you can't love her the way she is?

Over the years I've thought about her drool a lot, how it shines like a spider web, how it smells like baby's breath and sometimes puke, how it's like a clear window looking into people's hearts. It sparkles sometimes. I have dark stains on my shirts where she's drooled, pond marks that show where she fell asleep in my arms watching TV. Her drool is our own private history, and it's funny how something like that can become something beautiful, how it can bring people together.

It's just her and me now, after Rhonda left. She got tired of taking care of Mattie and went off with some punk in a rock band. She said she couldn't take it anymore. She said Mattie would be better off in a special home with other kids like her. She said she was too young to work and be a full-time nurse at the same time. She said all of this on her hands and knees, begging me to see it her way. She said we made a mistake and it was nobody's fault, that it was possible to move on, and that she loved Mattie but Mattie was eating away at our lives and that she wouldn't know the difference anyway. She questioned God and the genes in my sperm and her egg and how maybe there was someone like Mattie in her family history, but that it wasn't our fault. Mattie was a mistake and we did the best we could but there was no point in being miserable forever; we still had our lives to lead and places to go and how could we even take a day-trip somewhere without all these special preparations that just made us exhausted? I didn't know who was talking from the living room floor. Rhonda? Who is Rhonda? I didn't know anymore—and maybe I never did, until she broke down before me on her hands and knees as I sat in my chair with a beer in my hand.

I felt like I was falling through space, like the ground under me was ripped away and there was nothing left to keep me in place anymore. You could've drove a fire engine through my mouth. I watched Rhonda talk and I heard the words she was saying but they were like surf crashing on the shore or some kind of static that didn't make sense, and I felt dead inside, stone-cold dead, like everything I ever believed in was turned to ashes. Some things you never get over. I can't forgive Rhonda for abandoning us like that. I can understand it sometimes, but I can't forgive her. She took off when we needed her most, when I needed her to say we'd be all right even if she couldn't mean it. But I still miss her; I still ache for her body where the lace of her underwear meets her milky upper thigh and the way she smelled like hay tossed in the wind, which I can smell in Mattie's own hair sometimes. Still, I hope she rots in hell.

Mattie's glasses are bullet-proof thick, and she looks like that English scientist guy, Stephen Hawkins. I've seen pictures of him in his wheelchair with the sky set out behind him in glittering stars. I hear he's really smart. I hope he figures it all out someday—how the universe works, I mean. Mattie can't talk either, and she can't do any mathematical equations, but that's okay. She's twenty now, but has the brain of a small girl. Mattie's about four feet seven inches tall, if she could stand up on her own. She has a degenerative bone disease among other things, so she keeps getting smaller, shrinking almost, my daughter disappearing right in front of my eyes. We have to keep her strength up, keep filling her bones with calcium, or she'll just wither away. Her spirit is strong even if she can't put it into words.

Sometimes I think I can see right through her skin, it's that transparent. I see the map of veins on her forehead and it scares me; blue lines ray out like the roots of a tree. All that rushing blood in her tiny body, her head fragile like a tulip bulb. The thing is, she looks so smart, she looks like Stephen Hawkins, and I believe somewhere deep inside of her she is: she *is* really smart, only nobody, not even me, has ever brought it to the surface. I really believe that. She knows what's going on; I know when she feels safe and when she feels threatened. I know it like the feel of rain on the back of my neck.

When she came out of Rhonda I started crying my eyes out, not because she was deformed but because I was so happy to have a little girl, to finally be a dad. We knew soon enough what kind of child Mattie was, and that's when the problems started with Rhonda, the drinking, the arguments, the tears leading up to that scene in the living room. I lost three jobs and spent afternoons with Mattie in my arms, drinking beer and watching the sparrows dive and dip in the trees. That's when Rhonda started seeing the punk-ass rocker with gold hoops in his ears. He was some kind of pretty-boy singer and went after her bad. Right before Rhonda left I followed them one night, trailed them from bar to bar, where they came out holding hands and laughing like she had no care in the world, a husband and daughter who needed her, and after two hours I couldn't take it anymore; we came to a stoplight, I jumped out, and I started to whip the shit out of his face with my belt until he looked like some kind of bleeding Jesus. I could have killed him. But almost as soon as I started my rage went up in smoke and all I said was, "You two deserve each other."

You two deserve each other.

Only at night do I ever think of ending Mattie's life. I stand in the doorway with a pillow in my hands when I can't sleep, squeezing it, and I think how easy and merciful it'd be to put a pillow over her face and just end it, let her go. I don't mind any part of taking care of her, even when she makes a mess in her drawers; it doesn't bother me. But what if something happens to me? Who would take care of her then? That's when I get scared. I see what happens in those special homes: people left for hours in their wheelchairs, staring out the window because the staff is overworked and no one has the time. I can't leave her in a place like that. She'd wither and die—or worse, just hang on, hooked up to machines. She needs her own home, her own things. I tell her to squeeze the red rubber ball and she squeezes it. She knows how scared I am of what could happen. Her tiny fists clench in small spasms. They get even whiter at the knuckle until I think her bones are gonna stick through. I stroke her hair. We communicate through touches, like two balloons bumping into each other in a quiet room where nobody goes.

I stand in the doorway and I take a few steps into the room with the pillow in my hands and I think, *If this is some kind of sacrifice I don't know what it's for,* and my blood cries murderer, murderer, and whatever thoughts of mercy I had or blinding panic or fear, they all fall back and I start breathing like I just ran two miles. She's a tiny, frail bird glowing in the dark and I grow ashamed and frustrated because that's my big fear: what would happen to Mattie if something happened to me? I don't want to leave her behind to be abandoned and misunderstood. I hug the pillow to my chest, I feel my eyes get hot with tears. I'm tired of thinking about God; God-this and God-that, why does he do what he does, taking things and people away, warping them, the God-ways and the God-fear, and the bad stuff I try to hide away. I squeeze the pillow.

You don't say, "God, why did you give me this daughter who's deformed and retarded?" You don't say that. It doesn't even cross your mind. You don't wonder, why me, because it doesn't do any good. You want to be loved too, right? You want to be held and touched, right? You want someone to take care of *you*, right? Who's gonna do that for *you*? Who's gonna clean up your ass when you can't control yourself? Who's gonna hear you cry out in the middle of the night, breathing hard because you wake up and you're afraid? These are really important questions, man; nothing else matters. You don't want to be alone with no object around, no person who knows your name, knows that you even *are* a person. Some people think Mattie's a *thing*, something you're not supposed to look at, like she embarrasses them or gets in the way of dessert. Who are *they* to get all bent out of shape, to act like we just walked in naked or something, a traveling freak show?

In the circus of my dreams we're all like Mattie, and the seats are empty except for peanut shells. We're juggling for our lives and she's leading us in her wheelchair with a smile that lights up the tent. We're performing for our souls, and it's so important no one has time to make fun of anyone. And nothing else matters, not what we look like or how much we make or who's better than who because we're all equal under the tent, trying to keep in step with Mattie's directions, who waves her wand in her mouth to the rhythm of prancing tigers. And when we finally start moving together, the top of the tent rips open and all you can see is starry sky and night birds everywhere and Mattie is suddenly gone, to the place Stephen Hawkins is trying to figure out. She's disappeared into time, she's not pinned to her body anymore. Her chair is left in the dust, like a torture device in a museum. It's all a puff of glory, knowing my daughter is safe and cherished somewhere good. That's my dream of heaven. It makes the pillow thing almost seem worthwhile, an act of mercy, something she can at least depend on. God wouldn't strike me down for that; I know he wouldn't. He's not that kind of God, and if he is then fuck him, because I don't want any part of his so-called plan.

That's why I do what I do for her. Because she must know somewhere inside of her that I have this panic, that her dad has also plotted to kill her, has stood in the doorway in the middle of the night with his own blood whistling through his head, thinking panicky thoughts of what could happen if he's not around, who would feed her with her favorite Mickey Mouse spoon, who would tell her stupid jokes. It's not about me, it's about Mattie. All I think is, *She can't be left all alone, she can't be left alone*, a chant that follows me everywhere I go. I wake up sweating and then I stand in the doorway listening to her labored breathing with the help of a machine. Then it's that old place again, teetering on the edge of a black hole where there's no one to save me if I jump. It's misunderstanding I want to save her from, other people's horror of what they don't understand. If only I could communicate what this means, how invisible and dangerous this is, how if just one person in the world could really live in another person's skin how the whole damn mess would be revealed and you'd weep with sorrow and joy. Rhonda's the one who should be in that bed, learning once and for all what my daughter goes through. Then maybe her own hang-ups wouldn't be so bad and spread misery like a plague.

Once I had a stripper come to the house after dark when I thought I couldn't take it anymore, when I was beginning to think maybe Rhonda was right and that I'd never touch a woman again. I could hear Rhonda's desperate voice in the back of my head and it felt like a flood had broken, and was rushing all through me, and I wanted her back so bad I would have done anything. I kept asking, "When will this stop? When will I get some love?" Mattie was asleep and for once I didn't care if she was okay or not: I paced back and forth in the living room, the same living room where my ex-wife begged me on her hands and knees to get rid of Mattie, to do the only real practical thing and turn her over to people who knew what they were doing. Maybe Rhonda wasn't so heartless after all; maybe she was just exhausted and feeling that there was no way out, no hope, no relief. We did the best we could. This is the way it would always be, a lifetime of taking care of someone who couldn't even talk or hug us back, who couldn't control her own bodily functions; it was my turn to be touched, to be taken care of, even if I had to pay for it. And then I thought it, the one thought I've been trying to get rid of ever since, the one thought that will damn me:

You can't even say one word to your own father.

I made the call after my eighth or ninth beer. She was brunette and beautiful, with real faint freckles that made her look girlish and at the same time made her real sexy. I closed Mattie's bedroom door when I heard the doorbell ring, the only time I've ever done that. I didn't mess around. "Where do you want me to dance for you?" she asked, slipping off her tennis shoes and getting into high black pumps. I walked into the bedroom. "Dance for me in here," and I pointed at the floor, like we were going to dig a hole, and my voice was real gritty, like it wasn't my voice at all. She looked like a lawyer or a doctor in a long coat, and when she took it off I gasped. She had nothing on but a black lace bikini and high heels, and her breasts stood out from her body like they were their own set of low beautiful hills, and she set up her music box and told me to sit in a chair and get comfortable. Which I did.

I didn't think of Mattie at all. I didn't worry about her and I didn't care. I asked the stripper to turn the music down low and she did, and she moved above me, gyrating her hips like the most beautiful snake I have ever seen, straddling me, and leaned down in my face so that I thought her eyes were almost purple, and I could smell her perfumed hair and I almost passed out from grief or joy or relief, and she said, "Go on and touch yourself if you want," and I took my dick out of my pants, but it didn't do nothing, I couldn't get an erection, it just sat there like a flat tire. I wanted to get hard but I was so out of practice with a real live woman that her beauty stunned me and froze my blood. I couldn't move. I just followed the movement of her hips like they were a world rocking in space where the air is made of music and everything grows flowers or some kind of berry. She didn't ask what was the matter. She didn't say, "Aren't you attracted to me?" We just locked eyes and I fell into hers so far and deep and fast I felt completely lost in a good way, and then she said, "I'll help you," and took my shriveled dick and started working it. It took a long time, maybe a whole half hour, and when I came we were still looking into each other's eyes, and it was like I passed through an invisible wall where bliss had always been waiting for me on the other side, like an act of bitter forgiveness. I flooded myself and her hand and the whole chair and whatever defect that was in my sperm was out of my body now for me and her to see.

Then Mattie's alarm sounded in her room. I pushed the stripper back and fell to the floor, trying to get my pants up, but I was like a kid jumping on one leg in a gunnysack race, and the stripper asked,

"Where's the fire?" and I said, "It's my baby," and I was clawing at my pants and to her credit she helped me, she helped me get my pants on with sperm everywhere, and I ran down the hall and rushed into Mattie's room and there she was, swallowing her own tongue. I put my fingers in her throat and got it out. She was waving her arms back and forth like she was trying to balance herself. I got her tongue out of her throat and Mattie started wheezing real bad. She gasped for air like a delicate fish taken from the bottom of the ocean no one had ever seen before. I put her back on her respirator and cleaned myself up. But I didn't feel remorse. The stripper watched me from the doorway and it was her turn to be stunned, to wonder what the hell she'd gotten herself into. And really they were just two frightened girls, watching a big burly man with a gut sack clean up his daughter's puke and his own messed-up pants; I wiped off Mattie with a warm wash cloth and then I wiped off myself.

So this is it, I thought much later, *this is my life*, not with bitterness or regret or any real emotion just, *This is it*, like suddenly there was a cold bare mountain ahead of me and I had to climb it alone for the rest of my life, with Mattie strapped to my back. I paid the stripper and thanked her for helping me. I give her an extra-big tip. She said, "I'm really sorry, sir," like she was a schoolgirl after all, just pretending to be a stripper and occasional hooker. "Don't mention it. Don't give it another thought." Then she drove away in her little red Toyota.

There was this pickup truck parked like a block away on the street, and this long-haired guy was sitting in there all by himself, and he was staring at me. I stared right back at him. What the fuck was he doing there, anyway? It's not like me and the stripper didn't exchange anything the world doesn't see every day somewhere, two sad souls trying to take our minds off our troubles or earn a little extra money for law school. It's not like this was unusual, different, or far out from the normal course of things. And I just had this feeling that the guy knew all about it, that he had put two and two together and was just sitting there watching me in my own sad misery and secret joy. And I have to just stand there and watch him watching me for no good god-damned reason? So without giving it another thought I start walking over there. He couldn't know: I see children more handicapped even than Mattie. I see them being pushed around by other sad sacks like me, people who wear their hearts on their sleeves because their chests can't hold them in anymore, there's not enough room to feel all the joy and sorrow of raising a kid like this, and you don't have the energy to care what people think anymore. And who was he? Who the fuck was he to be watching me?

I used to take Mattie to the supermarket not just for groceries but because it was bright and there were people around—and it sure beat staying home night after night, watching the goddamned tube. You don't really know why people do the things they do. They might say they're looking for cans of mushroom soup but they might really be looking for love or relief or understanding, but there's no way to let other people know this—and who would stick around anyway if they did? Who would stop what they were doing and really give a fuck, not just some kind of weak lip service that sounds good but doesn't accomplish anything?

In Mattie's world, in my world, you do what you can to get by. You take crumbs, scraps, other people's jigsaw puzzles. You take hand-me-downs. You accept handouts without a word. You don't ask where you got something, you're just relieved you finally got it: a scarf, a touch, some attention, a chocolate kiss. Everything you do is connected to someone else's mood, if they feel like giving, if they can give you the time of day, if they feel sorry for you. Even someone opening a door is a gift you can't count on. You could be stranded by a mailbox for hours, you could get heat rash and die; you could be left in a mall with customers rushing around with shopping bags and none of them would see you, not even like a speck on the wall. Pride is a waste of energy. You dream of kites floating over the trees. You dream of train rides in the mountains with a beautiful person of the opposite sex who has googly eyes just for you, and you know, somewhere deep down and unbearable, that none of this will come true; your beating heart can't take the pressure of these false dreams anymore. Someone feeding you macaroni and cheese with a spoon becomes your favorite meal in the world, the focus of your day, something you look forward to out of all proportion to a meal in a box, this kid stuff staple. You want to dance, too. You want to pop wheelies. But really it's just getting across a room with the help of someone else that marks your life, that chains you to yourself.

So I walk over to this guy and neither one of us looks away. He's just sitting there in his piece of shit staring at me walking toward him, and him and me are gonna have some kind of conversation or reckoning because it's just unacceptable the way he's been eyeballing me. And you hear this—what?—shit, somewhere, where God says that the meek will inherit the earth, but all I ever saw was the meek getting the shit beat of them or just plain ignored, trampled underfoot like gum wrappers. But I'm not meek. I'm light-years from meek. I see the world through Mattie's eyes, and this is what I see: beauty in the smallest things, where you become an audience because you can't help it. A leaf. A piece of lint on your sleeve. Rhonda's laugh when we were still young and happy, with our whole lives ahead of us. Mattie sees a silver spoon in everything, never in a day of her life has she ever not awakened smiling. She smiles at everything, even when she's gagging on a noodle. I don't know how she can smile the way she does, when I see the world through her eyes, but she never stops smiling. Her teeth are like some crooked doors to paradise. For all my anger and fucked-up wrath, for all her ailments and pains, Mattie is somehow happy, and I don't know how this can be. How she can lay there like a doll, night after night, and coo in the dark like some well-fed pigeon. My daughter astonishes me. She doesn't have the hang-ups I have.

I say to the guy, "What the fuck you staring at?" and he doesn't look away. But then I get close enough and see who it is: it's him, that guy on the run who dug up that girl's body. And next to him in the passenger seat—I swear to God—is this little girl, and she's staring at me, too, only it was too dark and I couldn't see her before. But she doesn't look like any girl I've ever seen, and she's—what?—she's kinda glowing, and I stop dead in my tracks, I just come to a complete halt. And she, the girl, she just gives me this sweet, innocent smile, the most beautiful smile I've ever seen. And then they just drive away. They were in this neighborhood, and the girl wasn't dead, she was alive and she looked fine to me, radiant even. I didn't know what to do, how to react. Did they know what happened inside? Did they bless it somehow? But they were gone, and I thought about Mattie. She was in there, waiting for me, and I felt this flood of gratitude wash through me. I didn't want another life, another daughter: the truth was, I loved taking care of my daughter.

Because to her, everything is wonder. Her drool is the cleanest lake I know. Sometimes I look in her mouth and I see God looking back, and despite everything, despite the constant tiredness and the fear that she'll choke on her own blood or have a seizure, despite the overdue hospital bills and the possibility that Mattie won't live another four years, God is looking at me from the bottom of my daughter's mouth and he's blessing me with water, with Mattie's water, and for just a second I feel like the luckiest man on earth.

Lee Katz

I walk out of the 7-Eleven into the midday sun after playing video poker and losing three straight hands, and it's like stepping out of a dream-chamber with a jingle of change in my pocket. I spent my last five bucks on a pack of Old Golds and a cinnamon roll. I have stuff in the fridge at home, some apple juice and bread, some lunch meat. A can of won-ton soup. Cable's paid. I'm sixty and like to gamble. I have a taste in my mouth I can't get rid of, a slight metallic taste I always think of as the rim of an aluminum can. My car doesn't work. I'm free as a bird.

I eat the roll in the shade and jot down a few notes in the margins of a racing form, reminders of what I need to do and can't forget. Like call Chen to see how I made out last week, mail in the electricity bill, which is already overdue. Business matters, mostly. I came to Vegas twenty years ago after I left my second wife, who was pregnant at the time, for a would-be showgirl with a gap in her front teeth and skull-like knees, and I'm still here, on the make, scoring here and there in the desert. It's enough. You don't say, "I'm a small timer on the make living hand to mouth," or "I'm just one big score away from hanging it all up." No, you don't say that. What you say over and over again is, "Stay sharp, stay focused. Notice things." Now, if I could just quit smoking.

I like Vegas before dawn when the whole town hovers like a chandelier under water, so for just a moment you think it might float up into the atmosphere and disappear like it never was, and you watch the planes come in out of the sky like pins of light getting brighter and brighter on some guy's jazz piano, and you think *hell and paradise in one giant bowl*. You dream of coming here. You go your whole life in some dinky small town and think, *Vegas is a place where I could do the things I always wanted, become someone else, get away from everything. Forget New York and L.A., which are fine for your garden-variety freaks, out here you can become the genuine article, the guy who threw it all away on a hunch and keeps throwing it away on polyester suits and sports books because next to the seediness of it and the desperation of it he still has some great yearning lurking somewhere inside of him like a bright hidden god—he's still willing to risk everything.*

Can you see the beauty of this? Can you see how it makes your heart sing?

In the meantime you have frayed nerves, you're stressed beyond belief, things aren't working out wherever you're from, so you come out here. You go to bed in northern Minnesota and dream of stepping off the plane at McCarran and seeing all the empty space unfurl in dust devils to the canned chimes of the slots, sounding like a doomed cavalry of bells: you can't breathe, you wake in a cold sweat, so you light up in the middle of the night after another bout of insomnia, and suddenly Vegas pops into your head, like the last broken chance you'll ever get. That's how it works, how it clicks into place. Never mind what you'll do when you get here: the point is getting here at all, the stuff that went bad as you walk into a blizzard of fliers on the strip advertising buffet specials, exotic massages, 1-800 numbers for accident victims, foot rubs and a little nookie out at the chicken ranch where you drive for hours to the edge of nowhere, and find yourself staring up at a ceiling fan with rodeo tassels like the locks of someone's butchered hair. *What am I doing here? Who am I?*

You come here for the same reason I came: because you're desperate and you want another chance. You come because something is missing in your life and that something is you. You come because the days drip by like wet paint, because you're missing in action from your own life, because you want to fill up the days differently somehow, because you want to risk something and feel alive, because you wake in the middle of the night with your spouse next to you and the walls are closing in. The walls are always closing in. Sure, I know how it is. And Vegas is the opposite of that, sunshine and distraction and wide open spaces just outside the city limits, and maybe, just maybe, you'll have a few encounters with people you'll never see again. Do you think it could be any other way? *What if, what if* keeps haunting you at every turn, the two most seductive words in the English language—and it's a beautiful kind of haunting, the kind that opens doors in your mind.

I see them come out here, the wide-eyed ones, the cynical ones, the ones who can't sleep, the ones who will end up doing things they never dreamed of, leaving everything behind and running off with someone they hardly even know, getting hitched in Elvis chapels and riding sidesaddle on Harley Davidsons and wearing pearls, who blow every last buck they have, who have no chance of winning but keep playing anyway, who court losing like faithful Saint Bernards. How can a guy be better than Frank Sinatra unless the Frank we know and love never really was? Madonna? Who is Madonna? She doesn't exist.

I stand outside the 7-Eleven and smoke another cigarette. Have a sudden craving for a bagel with bits of sun-dried tomato, which I resist. Consider my options, which are nil. I spit out a kernel of cinnamon and it goes glutinous on the pavement. I light up again and smoke it down to the nub. I flick it into the hot, dry wind. I take the bus down West Sahara to the strip because this is the time of the month when I people-watch, when I'm flat broke and study the tourists with cameras strapped around their necks, gaping at the sights. I watch for the gleam of quarters and nickels on the sidewalk now because every cent counts. I study them, the busloads of people, tourists who have no clue, with their Hawaiian shirts and shopping bags and green visors like bank tellers from the Wild West, because it is the Wild West, the last frontier. Most of them walk around in running shoes. I sit on a bench outside Caesar's and watch them come and go. I notice the pink insides of their mouths. I see a stream of sunblock and plastic beads, idle chit-chat, posing for pictures. I can almost smell the vinyl seats in their cubicles back home in Des Moines or Toledo or West Branch, Texas, the desperation of their ergonomic plastic. I can see their bent and woebegone paperclips. It's like watching people who don't know they're about to step off a cliff. I wish they'd open their eyes and see what's going on, but maybe I'm fooling myself. Each drag of my cigarette gets more precious, and for just a second I feel like I'm going to break open like a box of Cracker Jacks and spill all over the sidewalk.

I'm looking for a flare of light in somebody's face. I'm looking for recognition. For no reason at all I stretch out my hand. I want to see if someone will touch it. They pass me by, ignoring it. I could be hitching a ride somewhere, I could be waiting for spare change. I want to see if someone will touch my hand and hold on, because it's out there. To brush it while passing by. To hold my hand in Las Vegas, for no other reason than because it's out there. My liver-spotted, trembling hand shot up with nicotine and too much bad coffee, a hangnail on my thumb and maybe some black ink—just an old guy's narrow wrist which keeps getting weaker and weaker. I dare you to take it, I dare you to see if it can be done. But almost always I'm invisible. Once, not too long ago, and despite the long odds, somebody actually did take my hand and hold on to it, a little girl with wavy chestnut hair who appeared out of nowhere, took my hand and smiled at me when I opened my eyes. Behind her and not too far away this long-haired and dangerous-looking guy was watching us. Only later did I learn who it was. And you know what? I hope they keep on going and never get caught. I hope people keep seeing them everywhere across the country because it gives them a little hope. Her touch was warm and electric in mine, and then she let go, the first and only time anyone's ever held my hand when I reached it out.

But not today. Today I lower my hand. I close my eyes and see orange. I think of Chen. He put me up when I first came out here. He's fond of paper lanterns. I don't know how old he is. He doesn't have a gray hair on his Asian head. I tell him it must have something to do

with the tea he drinks all day. He just nods and hacks, after taking another drag from his foreign cigarette. We understand each other. In the
early days Chen used to let me sleep on a cot in the back of his store.
It smelled like a box of unopened candles, waxy and mellow, like I was
about to be embalmed. A string of beads separated the rooms, like a
black woman's braided hair. I tried not to think of my wife and kids,
but sometimes they came rushing back anyway, on training wheels, in
the middle of a foggy meatloaf, a little red ball bouncing into a living
room tossed with hairy rugs. The blue vein running down Margo's De-
pression-like arm. I lay on the cot, hearing the soft kiss of billiard balls
where Chen played, and listened to big band music. I come to learn
a goddamn China man knows more about Benny Goodman than I
do. It was like we were both waiting for something to happen in that
cool dark place, something approaching from a long way's off, like a
whisper or a falling bomb. I strained my ears to hear it. I never cried in
Chen's place. I folded my hands across my stomach, like I was prepar-
ing for my own open coffin. But it was peaceful, not like I was sweating
bullets or anything.

The showgirl's name was Jodie, and she was just a kid who worked
at the local savings and loan. But we both had the same dream: to get
away and try something, anything else, and I used to flirt with her
every time I dropped off a check. I used to come under false pretenses,
with some prepared question or other, though we never had more
than two hundred bucks in the bank at any one time. Questions about
safety deposit boxes, about loans, about anything I could cook up to
talk to her. Once she took me in the back to see the vault and I heard
her panty hose make that static sound as she bent down to pick up a
pen, and right then I knew we would be in bed together in a month. I
just knew. I asked her, "Do you ever get sick of your life?" And she just
looked at me with those doe-kid eyes and said in a whisper, "In a really
bad way."

We left six weeks later with two suitcases between us and some plastic flowers I threw in the back seat. Two months after that she left me
in a cheap motel room with a single fly buzzing the ceiling. I never
saw her again. I guess I was her ticket out of Smallville, U.S.A. Next

to the bed was a half-filled bottle of Tanqueray and a split lime that had started to turn brown. I was the fly and the fly was me. God, was I thirsty. That's when I ran into Chen playing poker at the Sands. That's when I started to notice all the little pebbles getting into my shoes, pebbles so small they felt pulverized by a force that would crush anything that got in the way. All you hear and all you'll ever hear is how people come out here and have a streak of incredible luck, winning five hundred bucks here, hitting the jackpot there, getting set up for a night in the Bellagio for winning five, ten, or fifty grand, or just swimming in a waterfall of quarters. Meanwhile, there's me and Chen and a whole invisible army of worker bees who make this city hum. We're the flickering light in every neon bulb that blinks and goes out, blinks and goes out. Meanwhile, the losers keep quiet and don't say a word, because losing is silent anyway and doesn't have a voice. It's like tiptoeing across a bed of broken glass with your mouth taped shut. You take your beating without a peep as tiny hammer blows rain down on your aching shin bones and arms. Otherwise you betray the Dream, and if you betray the Dream you're worse than a snitch or a traitor, you're like someone who exposes himself to schoolchildren. Losers can only talk in the language of gum wrappers and trash bags blowing down the street; they can only talk in the tiny huts of crushed cigarette butts, in the green O of an empty Heineken rolling down the sidewalk, the hollowed out sound that doesn't have a name.

After awhile you sit on a park bench and hold out your hand; you walk out to the end of an invisible gangplank and step off, but you don't even fall; you close your eyes and think of the wife and kids you left with back payments due on everything and the peach colors coming through your eyelids like fuzzy navels and somewhere out in the desert a wisp of dust turns like a pipsqueak tornado and you think everything is leaving, everything is going away, even though you yourself are the one who left it all behind; everything is getting farther and farther apart and the molecules in your blood are moving away from each other like two magnetic poles pulling them in opposite directions, and you think *all that empty space*, and the funny thing, the real ha-ha of the matter, is that this growing empty space is getting bigger inside of you, wider and wider. Then you're not even a person anymore but something conscious and alive, hanging on to the last branch in the world.

I don't even know why Chen left China. We never talk about the past. We just sit and smoke and listen to records. He wipes off each one with a lint-free cloth and announces in a quiet accent, "Tommy Dorsey, 1944. You not know music like this before." And we sit and listen. Just sit and listen. I've never known a listener like Chen. It's like the music enters the lines of his face, softening them somewhat, they're like trenches that just decided one day to fold back into the earth again so they could grow lilies. Every hair on his head is always in the same place, like it was lacquered there at birth, like two perfect plates soldered to his skull. That's when I knew it is was impossible to know another person, that the best you could hope for were a few consistent mannerisms, a tick here or there, a bobbing and weaving sort of motion of the Adam's apple. He's not even a good bookie; I don't know where the hell he gets his money. He doesn't seem to know much about gambling one way or the other. I asked him once if he has the bones of his ancestors ground up in powder somewhere, and he just looked at me like I was crazy. "You not know music like this." I know that, Chen, don't you think I was listening? It's like Woodie Herman and the other hotshots of the era are his own personal gurus, they speak to him so quietly and so often that I really believe he can't hear anything else. It's like he was born to listen, only to listen. That makes for a cryptic friendship, if you ask me.

Say, Chen, what do you know about baseball, about the man on the moon, about Marilyn Monroe's last tragic days or the pouty way she comes on to every guy who looks at her posters? Blank stare. A few blinks. The guy doesn't even eat Chinese food. Who ever heard of a China man who doesn't eat Chinese food? "I no have use for it." Use? What does that have to do with food? I thought you people ate cats and dogs, you know, domestic pets. "I no like birds either." Do you think you could answer a straightforward goddamn question, Chen? "Clifford Brown, he play like he on borrowed time." I give up, shrug my shoulders. "Well, if you don't like Chinese food, I do; can I borrow ten bucks?" And he hands me a ten-dollar bill. Even though he'll never see it again. Even though I'm a lousy cardplayer. That's as close as he came to answering. I spend most of my time with a China man who won't answer one goddamn question I ask. It's a mystery to me. As far as I know he never steps foot out of the place. His entire life is three rooms, a record player, and a rotary phone that rings constantly though he never answers it.

Sometimes at night I think about what could have been, I think about the impossible. My fingernails are polished and groomed like clean windows to a monk's study. I pull up in a big red Seville with chrome hubs and honk in the driveway. The kids come rushing out and stop a few feet from the car. They've aged but they haven't. I recognize them but I don't. Their mouths are flung open in wonder, like gaping barn doors. I lower the window and my pinky ring winks in the sunlight. My eyes fill with tears. "Look in the trunk: it's all yours," I tell them. I pop the trunk. It hisses like air leaving a spaceship. I grip the steering wheel. They walk around slowly to the back of the car and I start to laugh. They pull out bundles of cash like it's play money, they pull out roller skates and cream pies and board games and furry gloves and college tuition and a pop gun and tickets to Disney World and everything they ever asked for which I couldn't provide, and I'm making a lake in the front seat, and "Wow, look at this," and "Gee, can you believe it," and then Margo comes out wiping her hands on a towel, looking tired and cautious and scared, and she asks, without any malice in her voice, "Lee?" and I grip the steering wheel tighter and tighter until I almost break my own skin, and I have only two words to say to her, two words that have taken a lifetime to muster and so much stupidity and waste, and I take a huge deep breath between sobs as she stands frozen in the driveway, I open my mouth, I raise up my bloodshot eyes to her, and I say, "Forgive me." Just that. "Forgive me." The kids squeal in delight. Margo doesn't move. I see Chen's sad eyes through the cigarette haze, dark and impenetrable as ever, the mysterious little girl who held my hand on the park bench, and her looming guardian. I can't read my wife's body language, I don't know what she will say. So before she says anything, before she even has a chance to speak, I crank up the volume on the radio, get out of the car, and get down on my hands and knees in my expensive summer suit and crawl toward her saying "Forgive me" again and again, over the sounds of my long-lost children laughing and the Glenn Miller band in full swing.

Der Abschied

Wherever you go now from now on, whatever street or field or country, whatever waiting room or office space, if you find yourself anxious and alone, trying to find the source of your wound, they will find you. They were waiting for you from the beginning, in childhood dreams you tried to forget, which return like figures coming out of the fog, in sudden hollows of loneliness where you wait at a counter for the prescription that will dull the edges of your pain, or a street corner where you suddenly feel overwhelmed by your own life, the years you've spent waiting for someone to rescue you, to find he or she is not coming after all. The times you composed letters in your mind that you will never write and never send, Dear Susie, Dear Bill, Dear Mom, Dear Dad, and the one strange day you recognize with dazzling clarity the singular beauty of a flower bud on the windowsill, blossoming in the sun.

What is the nameless thing that keeps following you, making you feel haunted, pursued, watched in a way that you can't describe? Why can't grace come back the way it came? Maybe you really are losing it this time, the nameless thing finally catching up with you after all this time, and evasions and dodges in the dark gaining like the shadow of a giant bird that will gather you up into its wings. You can't believe it's almost here and yet you've known it was never far away. Keep moving; don't slow down; don't look back. You've been running all your life, and now they are leaving you behind in the dust, panting, exhausted, out of breath. You can't keep up. The rising smoke of their departure is like incense announcing the end. It can't be any other way, your own life, in all its intimate details, its tiny hairs and moon-shaped scars, will never be repeated in all the scattered debris of the stars. Why do we try to forget this? They are coming for you across a vast distance, like the fervent prayer you say in the middle of the night when you can't sleep, looking for something, anything, to mitigate this knowledge: even the stained ideographs of leaves on the sidewalk are the glossolalia of your fate, but you can't decipher what they say.

One day you find yourself in a supermarket checkout line, staring at the tabloid faces and their chronicle of bathos and pathos and mass hysteria that constitute the clamoring world that will never love anyone and, fascinated, bewitched, filled with yearning for something else, anything else, you go into the lives of the people in the photographs, the grotesque, the unfortunate, and the celebrated, as if you are suspended in a glass tube:

Fattest Woman in the World Air-lifted from Her Bed
Christ Seen Imitating Elvis in Vegas Motel Room

And it suddenly hits you that you've wanted to believe in them all along, you've wanted to believe in the absurdities, the scandals, the UFO sightings, visions of Mary in oil stains at Jiffy Lube. You've wanted to believe that the supernatural is not supernatural at all, but commonplace and everyday, mundane as toast; that a dead girl really has been dug up by a janitor who took her and disappeared into the night to visit people no one would normally pay attention to: the damned, the warped, the misbegotten, those who would never otherwise show up on the news or in the *Wall Street Journal*.

You see his face, the one they call the Mover of Bones, and you see her, the way she looked before she was taken away, tortured, and killed.

For a moment you believe their story, you want to believe the accounts of levitation and rays of otherworldly light, you've waited for a story like this your whole life, for someone, anyone to redeem the emptiness you don't know how to describe, the emptiness outside the supermarket and the emptiness inside of you. It could be any dead girl, but it's her, Caroline Murphy; and he's the one, the one who found her, the Mover of Bones, who dug up her broken and dismembered body and sought a way to make her live again for people who could tell you what living again means. The headlines show the world is falling apart, unraveling in famine and war and suicide bombers, but for just a moment, for a second outside of time, you turn back to the pictures and story of the dead girl and you consent, you say it to yourself, in the deepest reaches of your heart, *I believe it. I believe every word.* Your heart skips a beat. The clerk scans the items of the old lady in front of you, who looks at each price on the screen like a bright-eyed bird. Then you feel it, and your blood surges with adrenaline:

Who will lead you out of the desert of your nameless longing?

The missing children are looking for you. They want you to take them back to where they used to be, in their own backyards, on the playground, on bedposts carved with their own initials. They are crying out with a voiceless plea, asking you to help them, to stop the pain and the darkness. They are coming for you. You see their faces on milk cartons, on fliers at the post office, stapled onto a telephone pole around the corner—and they look as if they have already disappeared into the void, someone's Bobby or Julie, haunting because they will always be innocent as you will never be again.

When they are taken away in the middle of the night, when they are persuaded to leave their bikes and swing sets, when their bodies cannot be found, who will continue to look for them when they are already dead? Will they always remain just a photograph, in smiles bashful and sheepish, forever captured in grainy dots of black and white, with blond hair and blue eyes and gap-toothed grins, with dark eyes and coarse black hair, in budding Afros and gleaming braces? Where are their bicycles, their G.I. Joes? Where are their huts made of backyard mud, the chalk they drew with on the sidewalk? You stand there in the checkout line. It's almost your turn. The old lady is writing a check with her veined and wrinkled hand, trembling over the book. Who would, who could, move their tiny dead bodies, the bones just beginning to grow? A thousand stories hit the stands like this every day, of burning forests started by careless campers, of chemicals killing birds in South America, of global mayhem, warfare, sex scandals, firemen rushing into burning buildings. But it's the dead girl and the man who dug her up that catches your eye and holds your attention, that burn into your heart. You move up in the checkout line, you use the plastic bar to separate your celery and soup and Life Savers from the person behind you, and you notice that the clerk scanning your items is tired and middle-aged, probably a single mother with kids of her own. Suddenly you feel that no matter what you do for the rest of your life, no matter how far you wander out of your way to find the cause of your own wonder and pain, you will never understand the kind of love that showers blessings on the bones of the dead.

University of Nebraska Press